CW00829300

CAMERON'S CONVOY

Further Titles by Philip McCutchan from Severn House

The Commander Shaw Novels

BLUEBOLT ONE
THE BRIGHT RED BUSINESSMAN
THE MAN FROM MOSCOW
MOSCOW COACH

The Donald Cameron Naval Series

CAMERON IN THE GAP

CAMERON'S CONVOY

Philip McCutchan

This edition published in Great Britain 1995 by
SEVERN HOUSE PUBLISHERS LTD of
9–15 High Street, Sutton, Surrey SM1 1DF.
First published 1982 by Arthur Barker Ltd.

Copyright © 1982 by Philip McCutchan
All rights reserved. The moral rights of the author have been asserted.

British Library Cataloguing in Publication Data
McCutchan, Philip
 Cameron's Convoy. - New ed
 I. Title
 823.914 [F]

 ISBN 0-7278-4771-6

All situations in this publication are fictitious and
any resemblance to living persons is purely coincidental.

Typeset by Hewer Text Composition Services, Edinburgh.
Printed and bound in Great Britain by
Hartnolls Ltd, Bodmin, Cornwall.

1

THE cold was appalling: it got into everything – deck gear, rigging, the breech-blocks of the guns, the very bone marrow of the suffering ship's company. Cameron, staring through binoculars at the merchant vessels and the other warships of the escort and on towards the hard, distant horizons, felt that the cold had entered his bloodstream and that his veins and arteries were filled with ice. Nothing could alleviate that cold, not even piping-hot cocoa brought from the galley by the boatswain's mate of the watch. Nothing, until dawn action stations was fallen out and the men not on watch could go below to the fug of messdecks and wardroom. Even that was a cold fug; the frigate's internal heating seemed never to cope adequately with the big freeze of the Archangel run, the Russian convoys.

At the fore guardrail of the bridge, the Captain was hunched into a duffel-coat, the hood of which was drawn half over his uniform cap, itself settled well down upon his ears. He spoke without turning.

'Number One.'

'Sir?' The First Lieutenant, Hawkey, had just come up the bridge ladder.

'Fall out action stations, resume cruising stations.'

'Aye, aye, sir.' Hawkey nodded at Cameron who, as navigating officer, took the bridge watch at action stations. Cameron passed the word to the boatswain's mate in the wheelhouse and waited for his relief, looking forward to getting some of the numbness out of stiff fingers. He yawned, steadied himself against the roll of the ship – currently there

1

was a dead flat calm, but the frigate felt as though it would roll in anything more disturbed than a dockyard basin. He listened to the boatswain's call piping round the upper deck, heard snatches of ribaldry as the gun's crews fell out. Weatherby, one of the RNVR sub-lieutenants, clattered up the bridge ladder to take over the watch while the Captain remained in his hunched position by the guardrail. Cameron was about to hand over when there was a shout from the starboard bridge lookout.

'Aircraft, sir, bearing red nine-oh. Looks like JU88s, sir.'

The Captain turned, bringing up his glasses on the bearing. He said, 'Belay the last order. Action stations again.'

Cameron reached for the button and pressed it. The alarm rattlers sounded urgently throughout the ship, sending men back to where they had just come from. The omens, he thought, were not good. They were little more than six hundred miles out from Loch Ewe, around three hundred east of Iceland and a hell of a long way to go. It was going to be worse than the frigate's last run, of which he had been told, graphically, by young Weatherby on joining. Weatherby had laid it on, all right: he'd survived a nightmare of attacks and sinkings, of men left struggling and gasping in the water, water that had been overlaid with a foul carpet of oil fuel from blown-up merchantmen, the sea erupting around them as thousands of tons of high explosive shattered the ammunition ships into white-hot fragments of metal that sizzled and peppered back from the skies. It hadn't sounded too bright; and this present run was to be Cameron's first experience of frigates.

Cameron had joined only a matter of days before; at the same time another officer had joined and he, too, had been about to make his first trip in a frigate. His first trip in anything smaller than a cruiser, as he'd said to Cameron when they'd met in a hotel in Thurso, awaiting the old ferry *St Ninian* that would take them across the Pentland Firth to Lyness in Scapa.

'Perishin' small stuff . . . I don't know!' Mr Fasher,

2

Gunner RN, had cast a critical glance at Cameron's two wavy stripes, the stripes of the RNVR. 'All reserves, so they told me. No offence, of course, Mr Cameron.'

'Of course,' Cameron said gravely. 'Where none is intended, none is taken. Naturally.'

'Eh?'

Cameron grinned. 'Never mind, Guns. Have a drink.'

'Thanks. Whisky. Keep the bloody cold out. Perhaps.'

Cameron ordered two whiskies. Mr Fasher elaborated. *Sprinter* was to be his first seagoing ship as a warrant officer. Until a few weeks back, he said, he'd been Chief Petty Officer Fasher, Chief Gunner's Mate of the parade in RN Barracks, Pompey . . . he didn't add that the barracks were only too pleased to see him go off to promotion and a thin gold stripe. Cameron remained unaware, but could have guessed, that Fasher had been an affliction, a dyed-in-the-wool product of the Whale Island Gunnery School, all gate and gaiters, the loudest voice Pompey had ever known. It had been said that even the Commander had had to deal tactfully with CPO Fasher if he didn't want all the seven thousand ratings in the depot to suffer from worn-down feet. Nobody mentioned the fact, but it was not unknown for nuisances to be promoted out of range and sent to crucify some unfortunate ship's company bucketting around the seas. Mr Fasher had the sort of face that went with crucifixion of his inferiors: beefy was the word. Raw, red beef covered with a look of truculence for gravy.

'Hands'll need knocking into shape,' he said, wiping the back of a big hand across his whisky-wet lips. 'Had it too soft, likely enough.'

'On Russian convoys, Mr Fasher?'

'Well . . . I didn't mean that, of course. I mean the discipline.' He almost said it in capital letters. 'Smartness, see?'

Cameron nodded. 'Yes, quite. That was why you were appointed, I expect.'

Fasher heard nothing sardonic. He said, 'Likely, yes.' He accepted another whisky, then said he had to go and write a letter to his wife. Before leaving the bar, he asked Cameron

3

what his own past experience had been, but he didn't seem to be listening to the answer, didn't seem to have noticed the ribbon of the DSC on Cameron's monkey-jacket. The RNVR didn't have experience, not to compare with his. Moodily, Cameron finished his whisky and then went up to bed. An early night might be a good thing; there wouldn't be too much sleep once he joined the *Sprinter* and they sailed from Scapa to pick up the convoy in Loch Ewe. Next day he and Fasher embarked aboard the *St Ninian* and moved out into the turbulent waters of the Pentland Firth where there seemed always to be half a gale blowing: Cameron's memories of the old *Carmarthen*, the destroyer in which he had done his lower-deck time, came back strongly. The Atlantic convoys had been murderous enough; by all accounts the Russian ones made them seem like child's play, especially in winter.

As the anchorage loomed up off Lyness Fasher identified the frigate. '*Sprinter*,' he said, and gave a snort. 'Misnamed, I reckon. Speed of a bloody tortoise, that's what she'll have. Know 'er vital statistics, do you, Mr Cameron?'

'No,' Cameron admitted.

'Should do. Right, I'll run through 'em.' Mr Fasher went off like a man auctioning a catch of fish. '1,435 tons displacement, official speed twenty knots and like I said that's bloody likely I don't think, two four-inch guns, four two-pounders, six 20mm, Asdics, complement one 'undred and fourteen officers and ratings. Right?'

'If you say so, Guns,' Cameron said, grinning.

They waited on a cold, wind-torn jetty after Cameron had caused a signal to be sent to *Sprinter* from naval HQ, asking for a boat to bring off two officers joining. A motor-boat came in under the charge of a leading seaman, oilskinned and sou'westered. Mr Fasher clambered down to the stern-sheets and Cameron followed. They sat on a thwart beneath a canvas canopy; Fasher looked around, wrinkling his nose. The boat could do with a bit of spit-and-polish in his view: the brasswork showed verdigris.

'Who's the skipper, lad?' he asked the coxswain.

4

The leading seaman said, 'Lieutenant-Commander Stanford, sir. RNR,' he added informatively.

'Love-a-duck,' Mr Fasher said. 'First Lieutenant?'

'Lieutenant Hawkey, sir. RN.'

'We'll get on,' Mr Fasher said. RN suited him fine, since that was what he was. He'd seen it all, the Service in its great days before the reserves had come along to dilute it. Battleships, battle-cruisers . . . he'd served as gunner's mate in the *Queen Elizabeth*, flagship of the Mediterranean Fleet, in the *Renown*, in the County Class cruiser *Devonshire*, and then as Chief Gunner's Mate in the *Malaya*. What he didn't know had yet to be dreamed up.

'Bloody Fasher,' Leading Seaman Holloway said later in the seamen's mess-deck when the motor-boat had been hoisted and secured for sea behind the broad canvas swathes of its gripes. 'Just my luck. We've met before. Anybody else know the sod?'

No-one present did. *Sprinter* was manned largely from the Devonport Port Division. Holloway went on, drinking cocoa, 'More bullshit than any field I ever see. We can all watch out now – I feel sorry for the poor bloody gunner's party,' he added in reference to the seamen detailed to assist the gunner and the gunner's mate in looking after stores and equipment and ammo and in keeping the guns themselves in perfect working order, ready for anything at any moment. Holloway knew something about Fasher that Fasher didn't know he knew; it involved a good friend of Holloway's, a young petty officer who'd had a promising career ahead of him until he'd come up against the then Chief Petty Officer Fasher. . .

'Did he recognize you, Killick?'

Holloway looked across at the ordinary seaman who had asked the question. 'Grow up, Lofty. I was just an AB, one o' bloody thousands. And happy to be it, nice and anonymous, when Jingo Fasher was around.'

'Jingo?'

'That's right. Bravest bugger not afloat – like the barber's cat, Lofty, full of wind and piss.'

5

Cameron, steel-helmeted now and dodging down into the lee of the bridge screen as the JU 88 screamed over the frigate, then coming upright as the spitting cannons veered away to give some respite, manoeuvred the frigate to port and starboard as Stanford passed the orders to avoid the sticks of bombs. *Sprinter* heeled, almost coming gunwale-under on the turns. Stanford stood like a rock of defiance, handling his ship calmly and expertly even though she was a very different kettle of fish from those he'd been used to in his Merchant Service days: three-island, general cargo vessels of the Clan Line, trading world-wide and carrying up to twelve passengers. After some years as Chief Officer, he'd made Master just before the war broke out. As his close-range weapons stuttered away at the enemy aircraft he was thinking of his wife in Southampton, living through something similar. They'd been a happy and united family, though he saw too little of them in between long voyages to Australia, India, America. Three children, all boys, who'd intended following him to sea in the Merchant Service, all meaning to become master mariners. Two might, given time and the chance to live – they were at school near Southampton. One wouldn't; the German bombers had seen to that just four months earlier. Stanford had been at sea and when he got back the funeral had taken place. Mary, he believed, would never get over it. Nor would he, but he had plenty to occupy his mind and keep thought at bay. The war had now become very personal to him. The more Germans he could kill, the better. He was untiring in his efforts in that direction: the ship's company, his ship's company, had been exercised and trained to a high degree, not far off the elusive goal of perfection. This he knew; so did the whole complement, officers and men. True, there were shortcomings due to the inexperience of one or two of his junior officers and of some of the newly-promoted petty officers, but this would be cured by time and by more and more exercises and indeed by action itself. Every day brought some improvement in, for instance, the time taken to close up at action stations and the time

6

taken to open fire; and in the efficiency of his Asdic team, one of his principal weapons. *Sprinter* was of recent construction and had been fitted not only with the latest A/S equipment but also with radar, the latter not even now by any means available to all warships.

It was this knowledge of efficiency that had caused him to react badly to his new gunner. On being introduced to his Captain, Fasher had been condescending. Stanford had expressed the simple hope that Fasher would soon get accustomed to life aboard a frigate. 'Not what you're used to,' he'd said with a friendly smile.

Fasher had appeared to sniff. 'No, sir. Not . . . *quite*, no.' He'd quoted a battleship or two, plus Pompey barracks. His beefy face and mean eyes had looked obstinate, as though he had already decided not to like frigates. Then he'd said, 'The 'ands'll need to be smartened up, sir. They're scruffy.'

'I'm sorry about that, Guns,' Stanford had said. 'They've been at sea, you know.'

'No excuse, sir, isn't that. Any man can wash and shave and wear 'is uniform proper.'

Stanford had said, 'I see. Well, in that case, Guns, I suggest a word with Number One.' He had been unable to resist adding, 'He's RN too.' That had been a mistake; he'd seen that in Fasher's face: the skipper, Fasher had obviously been thinking, is a touchy so-and-so. The real truth had been that Stanford was half-way to being worn out both physically and mentally from the sheer strain of a long war and continual convoy escort duty, which shattered men as it shattered ships, and Fasher had got him on a raw spot.

As suddenly as it had begun, the attack ceased. Stanford watched the aircraft flying away and vanishing over the horizon. His ship had suffered no casualties this time, but this was just the start. They would scarcely get through and back without losing some men. Last run they'd lost far too many: one had been the gunner, hence Fasher; another had been an RNR lieutenant, hence young Cameron. Ordering the hands to fall out once again from action stations, Stanford studied Cameron for a few seconds before the crusing-station reliefs

7

came up. The DSC spoke for itself; Cameron had a good record from all his previous ships and there was about him an air of reliability under pressure. That was good; there was going to be plenty of pressure from the Germans. They would do their best to stop this convoy getting through – they surely must. Quite apart from certain other considerations of which the German High Command might or might not be aware, the cargoes would bring much needed assistance to keep the allied Russian armies fighting.

Before going into the wardroom for breakfast, Cameron braved the cold for a little longer to look out at the convoy from the quarterdeck. The destroyers of the escort were reforming after their repulse of the aircraft attack, steaming at speed into their positions around the merchant ships, leaving wide swathes of disturbed water behind them, leaving *Sprinter* to resume her station as arse-end Charlie, well astern. The signal lamps were winking out messages between the Commodore of the convoy, the Senior Officer of the escort, and Captain(D) in the destroyer flotilla leader. This was an exceptionally heavy escort: in addition to the destroyers and frigates, HMS *Belfast*, a cruiser of ten thousand tons carrying twelve six-inch guns in triple turrets and strong batteries of anti-aircraft armament, and HMS *Durham*, another heavy cruiser, had come out from Reykjavik to join the escort soon after the convoy from Loch Ewe had raised Iceland; somewhere in the vicinity Admiral Sir John Tovey, flying his flag in the battleship *King George V*, was at sea with the Home Fleet acting as a shadowing force available to join at speed should any heavy German units be reported. The convoy itself consisted of no less than thirty-six ships, most of them big ones. Seven of them carried ammunition, ten were loaded with field guns and tanks, anti-tank guns and machine-guns. Another seventeen carried an assortment of war material such as radar and radio equipment and telephone sets, industrial machinery, food-stuffs, medical supplies and hospital equipment, plus raw materials for the Russian factories. Since the destroyer escort

8

and the cruisers were under orders to return with a westbound convoy and would not be entering harbour at Archangel, two re-fuelling tankers of the Royal Fleet Auxiliaries – *Oligarch* and *Black Ranger* – were accompanying the convoy, forming, with their escorts, Force Q.

Cameron turned as he heard the door in the after screen come open. Weatherby emerged, round and smiling, cherubic: until the war had started he had been a bank clerk and a good one. Now, in addition to his executive duties as a sub-lieutenant, he acted as Captain's secretary dealing with the correspondence and paperwork. Bumph was inseparable from war.

'Morning,' he said cheerfully. 'Glad we're still here after that lot.'

'Do you normally get it so early on?' Cameron asked.

'No, we don't. It's been known, but it's usually farther along.' Weatherby waved a hand around the concourse of ships ploughing their furrows through the water. 'We've got value – more than usual. It's not only all that lot, either,' he added mysteriously, then seemed to realize he'd spoken out of turn. He said, 'That's not for broadcasting. I never said a word. Father's going to speak to the ship's company during the forenoon.'

He went on along the upper deck. Cameron went in through the after screen towards the wardroom. Hawkey, the First Lieutenant, was at breakfast and was talking to Fasher, at the same time giving a broad wink at Leyton-Seton, the second of the RNVR sub-lieutenants. Cameron grinned inwardly. Hawkey might be RN like Fasher, but it was a pound to a penny that Hawkey found Fasher less *simpatico* than Leyton-Seton. Leyton-Seton had been at Eton. There was quite a jingle about that thought.

2

THE aircraft came in again, many of them this time. From the bridge Cameron counted twelve, coming in out of the sun, the sun that blinded but did little to warm. A heavy concentration of anti-aircraft fire went up from the escorting ships and once again the signal lamps were busy. The sky was filled with small white puffs, with aircraft that buzzed and hurtled, crossing the convoy to rake the decks with machine-gun fire. As *Sprinter* increased speed to come closer to the convoy, spent cartridge-cases rattled about her decks. Fasher seemed to be everywhere at once; from time to time his raucous voice could be heard even above the gunfire. Like Fasher, sound was everywhere too, battering at the ear-drums, the cacophony of war. As bombs came down waterspouts rose around the onward-plodding ships. Bows emerged through heavy spray, dogged, determined. Two of the JU 88s were hit; one exploded in the air, the second lost height with black smoke pouring behind, then took the sea in a great splash. For a moment a man could be seen trying to crawl out along a wing, then the aircraft vanished and the German with it.

Fasher's voice was heard, loudly. 'Bastards! That's the stuff to give 'em.'

On the bridge the Captain said, 'What we need is a carrier.'

Cameron made no answer; the time might come when the convoys would have carrier protection, but for the present the great floating airfields were needed in other war theatres and they had to go without. There simply were not enough to go round, though rumour had it that the United States might

10

supply, on a lease-lend basis, a number of smaller aircraft carriers to be known as escort carriers. If that came about, then the convoy picture would alter considerably.

'Hard a-starboard,' the Captain said suddenly.

'Hard a-starboard, sir.' Cameron passed the order down the voice-pipe to the coxswain in the wheelhouse; phlegmatically, Chief Petty Officer Murdoch brought the helm over; *Sprinter* lurched heavily, coming round just in time. A stick of bombs came down in the water and a series of waterspouts rose to throw spray over the frigate's decks; and almost simultaneously one of the merchant ships was hit.

The Captain steadied the course and lifted his glasses. He said, 'It's the *Loch Carron*. General machinery. And I believe she's going. Port fifteen.'

'Port fifteen, sir.'

'Seaboat's crew and lowerers. Stand by scrambling nets.'

Cameron bent to the the voice-pipe, passing the order to the boatswain's mate. The *Loch Carron* was ablaze from stem to stern and was well down by the head already. As the frigate's seaboat was slipped men were jumping into the water. The Captain took *Sprinter* in towards the stricken merchantman and when he was close he stopped engines to drift up to the swimming survivors. The rescue operation was efficiently conducted so far as it went: *Sprinter* and her company had seen it all before, too many times. The survivors, some from the seaboat and some who had grasped the scrambling nets to come aboard like wingless flies, were made as comfortable as possible below decks, where they were seen by the Surgeon Lieutenant and his sick-berth attendants. *Sprinter* had picked up thirty-one men. Upwards of twenty were unaccounted for, including the Master and most of the engine-room complement.

Before the German attack withdrew, another ship had gone, another cargo lost to Russia, another tally of dead and wounded. The rest steamed on, chivvied by the escorts who were in turn chivvied by Captain (D) in the leader. The war had taken its toll; many of the watchkeeping officers in the destroyers and frigates suffered from a lack of experience.

The Navy was now rather more than ninety per cent RNVR as regards its commissioned ranks.

Fasher remarked on the point to Hawkey as the two officers made a tour of inspection of the guns. He said, 'It's a reservists' war, now, sir.'

'None the worse for that, Guns.'

Fasher gave a snort. 'You an' me, we're RN. Active Service, what's more.' The reference was to the fact that they were neither of them retired pre-war, neither of them were dugouts recalled in 1939. Naturally, everyone was on Active Service, but recalled pensioners were, by use of that subtle 'Active Service' with capitals, excluded; at any rate in Fasher's mind. Men like Chief Petty Officer Murdoch, who was an RFR man, a fleet reservist brought back from his greengrocer's shop in Devonport, once again to serve the King. Many others were the same. Fasher went on, 'Just the two of us, in the wardroom. Plus the warrant engineer, of course. Stiffening, I calls us.'

'You'll find the *Sprinter* doesn't need that.'

Fasher sniffed; as a newly-promoted warrant officer he wasn't going to stick his neck out so far as to argue the toss with Jimmy the One, not yet anyway, but what Jimmy had said sounded like complacency and that would never do. As all that was present of the RN, the straight stripers – and never mind that his own was just a thin one – they should stick together. Not that Mr Hawkey was Dartmouth trained, he wasn't. He'd joined by the public schools entry, what they called Special Entry, a year or two before the war. Murdoch, the coxswain, had told Fasher that on being asked. Fasher had suspected it; there wasn't quite the Dartmouth touch. Call it a lack of arrogance, perhaps, a lack of total certainty that all he did was right. Just the same, he was RN and as such had to be regarded as nicely dried out behind the ears.

There was a let-down coming. Hawkey put a finger on a nasty fault: a small patch of rust on the breech block of Number One gun for'ard. 'See that, Guns?'

'Yes. I see it. It'll not be there long, sir.'

'Just call me Number One, Guns. We're not being all that formal. And get the rust removed, will you?'

'I just indicated I would.'

Hawkey grinned. 'My apologies!'

'And I'll say this if I may. I've not been aboard long. That's not meant to be an excuse. It's just to say that now I *am* aboard things is going to be different.'

'Not too different if you're wise – which I'm sure you are. We're not a bad ship's company and we pull together pretty well. Father runs a good ship and a taut enough one to be happily efficient. When I was in the *Ark* . . . I found out just how good a happy ship was, Guns.'

'Oh, yes,' Fasher said non-committally. The coxswain had told him something else, offered as a warning: practically every time Jimmy opened his mouth he started off by saying 'When I was in the *Ark*,' the reference being to his commission in the carrier *Ark Royal*, in which he had been gently sunk off the Gibraltar Strait. The old *Ark* had settled like a motherly hen, giving everyone bar one man ample time to get off after she'd been torpedoed. When Jimmy was called away by the skipper, Fasher was left to reflect that he'd been given a tactful rebuke, a sort of rebuke in advance, and he didn't like that. He was not accustomed to being rebuked, anyway not since he'd been a snotty-nosed OD. From then on, he'd gained promotion by taking good care not to incur rebukes. He took a turn or two up and down the fo'c'sle, stepping with care over cables and Blake slips, bottle-screw slips and coamings, teetering a little to the ship's motion, what he regarded as a bloody awful roll such as had never been produced by the battleships or battle-cruisers. He had already remarked on this to the buffer, who had retailed the conversation to Dusty Miller, the Petty Officer Telegraphist. Miller had said that Pompey parade ground didn't roll much either, but Fasher was unaware of this remark.

He went back to Number One gun.

'You,' he said. 'Captain o' the gun.'

Leading Seaman Trott turned and saluted. 'Yes, sir.'

'Breech block's falling to bloody pieces, Trott.'

Trott looked astonished. 'Is it, sir?'

'If I say so it is. Rust! Remove it and remove it fast.'

'Aye, aye, sir.'

'It's there.' Fasher jabbed a finger on the spot indicated by Hawkey. The spot vanished. Fasher looked at his finger: it wasn't rust, it was blood. A carelessly-closed breech-block had nipped flesh. . . there was a faint grin on Trott's face. Fasher's beefy visage went a deep red. 'Take that smile off of your face, Leading Seaman Trott, or I'll lose you your rate. Blood shouldn't be there any more than rust. The First Lieutenant saw it himself. You'd best watch it . . . like I'll be watching you.'

Trott said afterwards to Leading Seaman Holloway that bloody Fasher hadn't been able to wait to let him know it had been Jimmy who'd made the mistake, not himself. Holloway wasn't surprised. Typical Fasher, he said. If the spot had been rust he'd have claimed for himself the credit for spotting it. There had been a cock-up once, in RNB, when the seamen divisions had ended up milling about the parade ground in bloody great heaps. Fasher had made it clear that the fault lay with one of the petty officers when in point of fact some aberration had led him into mistaking right for left. Holloway said something else as well, only partially relevant: Jimmy the One was beginning to need glasses and never mind that he was only in his twenties. Holloway had noticed a lack of vision on more than one occasion, but reckoned that Jimmy wouldn't ever admit to it in case he got a medical board and had to go ashore for the rest of his service.

At four bells the tannoy was switched on from the bridge and Stanford spoke to the ship's company. He said, 'This is the Captain speaking. You may be wondering about the strength of the escort, which is unusual. I can explain that. In the first place we are escorting an exceptionally valuable convoy.' He ran through the list of the cargoes, stressing how much the Russian armies needed the war materials in their fight to keep Hitler away from Moscow. Then he said, 'There's something else. A human cargo, and this is the particular reason why it's

14

expected we shall come under very heavy attack as we approach the North Cape – or before.' He paused. 'The convoy's carrying two very important persons. One of them is a British cabinet minister, the other is a Russian general. It's vital that they get through. I've not been told which ship they're in, none of the commanding officers of the escort has been told that. My guess at the reason is this: if an obvious concentration of defence is made on one ship, it'll be a giveaway to the Germans. Besides which, we still have the whole convoy as our shared responsibility, not just one ship. That is all.'

The tannoy clicked off. There was a buzz of conversation throughout the ship. Cameron knew, now, what Weatherby had bitten back his tongue on. Taking a stand-easy in the wardroom over a cup of coffee, he caught the eye of Leyton-Seton, who was lounging with his long legs dangling over the arm of a leather-upholstered chair. 'I wonder what the cabinet bloke's going to do,' he said.

'Not our worry, old boy.' Leyton-Seton slipped a cigarette into a long green holder. 'We just go on suffering all this bloody interminable hardship. Two VIPs won't make any difference to that, though I take Father's point about attack.' He frowned. 'There's one thing, though.'

'What?'

Leyton-Seton blew smoke across the wardroom. 'I hope history doesn't repeat itself. In the last war, Kitchener was en route for Moscow in the *Hampshire* . . . and *he* was sunk and drowned.'

Kitchener was mentioned on the lower deck as well: sailors had long memories and many among the older hands, Fasher's fleet reservists, could recall the sinking of the *Hampshire* only too clearly. Kitchener had been England's hero then and there had been national alarm at his loss. A Field Marshal, Secretary of State for War at the time, in a sense a general and a cabinet minister rolled into one. As Holloway remarked as he made a fag from a tin of Tickler's, times had changed and maybe today the loss of a VIP wouldn't create so much stir; hero-worship was a thing of the

15

past except in one instance and it wasn't likely Winnie was in the convoy. On the other hand, the Nazis had a very strong and basic belief in the cult of leadership. They could well believe Britain had the same outlook: the Nazis hadn't proved too clever in assessing the British character so far. Sure, it sounded like an invitation to attack – if the Nazis knew the VIPs were in the convoy. The skipper hadn't been specific on that, and naturally the secrecy would have been intense, but secrecy could never be relied on. Be Like Dad, Keep Mum looked fine on the posters, but there were still too many loose tongues around. Of course, a lot depended on just who the cabinet minister and the Russian general were. Suggestions varied from Beaverbrook and Timoshenko, who might have left the Russian front for some vital mission, to Sir Stafford Cripps or Attlee plus almost any Russian general the particular speaker happened to have heard of. None of them quite came up to Kitchener.

'I've not been told who they are,' Stanford said. He had left the bridge, instructing Weatherby, the Officer of the Watch, to sound the alarm rattlers instantly if anything hostile, or likely to be hostile, should be sighted. He had called a conference in his cubby-hole of a sea-cabin: Hawkey and Cameron were the only others present, which was just as well spacewise. These two were Stanford's next senior officers and there was something his second-in-command should know, in case he himself became a casualty. And, for a similar reason, it was better to split the information three ways rather just two while he was about it.

He said again, 'I've not been told who they are but I've been left in no doubt at all that if they don't reach Archangel, the course of the war is likely to be shifted against the Allies. Of course, the basic responsibility for their safe arrival rests with the Senior Officer of the escort, but it so happens we ourselves have a very special part to play. That special part won't begin till we reach Archangel. You already know, of course, that although the destroyers and the *Belfast* and the *Durham* are detaching to pick up the westbound convoy,

16

Sprinter is under orders to enter the port. Well, that'll be the start of it.'

Stanford unlocked a drawer beneath the bank and brought out a buff envelope marked with the security classification HUSH MOST SECRET, the top classification of all. He said, 'You both understand this goes no further?'

Hawkey and Cameron nodded.

'Then I shall pass it to you both in turn,' Stanford said, and handed a single sheet of typewritten Admiralty-crested paper to the First Lieutenant. Holding the paper away from his eyes, Hawkey read:

To Commanding Officer HMS *Sprinter*.
1. The two persons to be embarked in the forthcoming PQ convoy the escort of which you will be part will be conveyed safely to Archangel.

Having read thus far, Hawkey looked up with a grin.

Stanford laughed. 'That's your service, Number One! Things "will be done" and never mind the opposition – or just bad luck! However, go on.'

Hawkey went back to the orders. They were stark.

2. These persons will be transferred aboard *Sprinter* from the convoy as soon after berthing as expedient. This will be done in secrecy. It is known that a number of enemy agents are active in Archangel.
3. Following the arrival of the persons aboard *Sprinter* you will proceed to sea with the next westbound QP convoy.
4. When you are well clear of Archangel you will alter course to enter Murmansk and prepare to land the two persons. Further orders will reach you on arrival.
5. You are reminded of the over-riding need for full secrecy and of the relevant paragraphs in the Articles of War referring to disregard of orders.
6. You will not construe the preceding paragraph as in any way whatsoever relieving you of a commanding officer's duty to use his initiative when required by the exigencies of the service to do so.

That was all. The document carried no signature, the name or rank of no originator beyond the Admiralty crest. Hawkey passed it to Cameron, then looked up at the Captain.

'Someone,' he remarked drily 'isn't all that anxious to assume any responsibility at all.'

Stanford nodded. 'Typical of the Admiralty is that. We just have to live with it. As there's that lack of a signature, I suppose I could plead no orders if things go wrong – but they'd still have my head on a charger. The one I like,' he added, 'is para 6!'

'Initiative – yes. They have you all ways up, sir. But again, they always do.'

'Damn right.' The Captain looked as if he was about to add something further when the strident note of the alarm rattlers sounded, making the tooth-glass jiggle and sing in the rack above his wash-basin. 'Here come some more of the buggers,' he said. As Hawkey and Cameron doubled away to their action stations, he locked the buff envelope back in the drawer, then ran out behind them carrying his steel helmet. As he ran for the bridge he was thinking about the way the Admiralty covered itself. The whole damn place, he thought, was cocooned in defensive paper armour, converting itself into a sort of bumph-turret from which issued, not projectiles, but equally lethal *double entendres* and orders that conflicted one with another so that in effect everything was left to the man on the spot and whatever that man did was fifty per cent likely to be wrong.

Stanford reached the bridge. He found Weatherby looking crestfallen. 'Where's the enemy?' Stanford asked.

'False alarm, sir. Sorry, sir. I thought I saw a speck against the sun.'

'I doubt if the off-watch men trying to sleep will appreciate it, Sub, but not to worry.' One couldn't come down too hard on somebody doing his best.

'Thank you, sir.' Brightly the sub-lieutenant added, 'Better safe than sorry, sir.'

Stanford grunted. That was the sort of thing Weatherby would say: he was somewhat predictable. But at least he was alert and had the makings of a good watchkeeping officer and that was the main thing. Having come back to the bridge, Stanford remained there. He would probably be there right the way through to Archangel, night and day, leaving only for short spells of essential sleep in his sea-cabin. Same as last voyage, and the one before, and the one before that . . . it was always the same on convoy duty, things happened very fast. Behind his duffel-coated back, Weatherby studied him thoughtfully. Weatherby was still finding life strange; the sea and its followers, the professional ones like the Captain and Hawkey, and now Fasher, he found vaguely disturbing and very different from his former colleagues at the bank. Captains were a far cry from managers of banks and inclined to be a good deal more forthright, though at times they could relax and be friendly without losing discipline. Bawl you out one minute, crack a joke the next. Bank managers in Weatherby's experience tended to be formal at all times. Then there was the difference between the two sets of professionals, RN and RNR. Weatherby couldn't quite put a finger on that difference, but it was there. It was there even in young Kelly, the eighteen-year-old Midshipman RNR who acted as general dogsbody and took a bridge watch as second Officer of the Watch with Number One. Kelly was a rum 'un to some extent who didn't quite fit in with RN ways and when it came to things like gunnery and the day-to-day exercise of naval routine he sometimes seemed as lost as Weatherby himself felt; but he was all about when it came to being on the bridge, more so than Hawkey in fact. On the bridge he had a kind of self-containment, an inner knowledge that perhaps came with plenty of sea experience. Even Kelly had done four years at sea as an apprentice in the British Tanker Company and had been about to sit his examination for Second Mate when war broke out and a few months later he'd joined the RNR. He already had as much sea time in as the First Lieutenant. The RN brand of efficiency was a different one and again Weatherby found it hard to define. All he knew, in a humble sort of way, was that he had yet to attain either variety himself and he doubted if he ever would.

19

Leading Seaman Holloway was off watch and should have been sleeping but he wasn't. He was dead tired but couldn't sleep; and he had things to do. He was sitting at the mess table below the swinging hammocks of those who could and did sleep, and he was working away at a piece of wood that was beginning to take on the rough outline of a warship.

Three months earlier Holloway had been serving in a cruiser, HMS *Argyll*. She'd been employed on the Northern Patrol, watching over the northern exits to the Atlantic, between Iceland and the Faeroes and around the Denmark Strait. When earlier in the war the rest of the cruisers had been withdrawn on replacement by liners converted into AMCs, the old *Argyll* had been left, for she was very old and worn out and would have been little use in any other theatre of operations. So she had maintained her patrol, sometimes at sea for weeks on end, running up and down her allotted area, crossing and re-crossing the dreary turbulence beneath largely leaden skies. Mostly it was monotonous routine with not much happening; and Holloway, with time on his hands when off watch, had made many friends, close friends as such men become within the confines of a ship at sea: either that or you hated their guts, one or the other. There was something about long periods at sea that made that happen, but there hadn't been many men, ever, that Holloway had hated. Then three months ago the *Argyll* had steamed slap into the great turreted guns of a German pocket-battleship heading out for the South Atlantic by way of the Denmark Strait and she'd bought it. The Jerry's first salvo had carried away the *Argyll*'s receiving and transmitting aerials, her second had blown the stern off and the third had taken her amidships, the two together blasting the engine spaces out of existence. Leading Seaman Holloway, who had the non-substantive rate of seaman torpedoman and was at his action station at the tubes amidships, had been blown clear overboard, along with a number of other men.

It had been sheer luck that he hadn't frozen to death. So many people had never survived immersion in those northern waters. A Carley float had been blown clear with him, taking the water close, and he'd scrambled into it and paddled towards the other men struggling in the icy sea. He'd pulled three of them aboard and then within minutes a British battleship had appeared through an encroaching fog bank – luck again: the firing had been heard. The German had turned away under full helm and vanished into the mist, and Holloway and the three men had been picked up. In the interval the *Argyll* had disappeared in a cataclysmic explosion and a massive cloud of smoke and escaping steam. Holloway and the three others had been the sole survivors. The cold sea had dealt with the rest.

He could see it all still. His hand shook a little as the knife approached the wood that he was carving, but steadied as contact was made. He carved slowly, with infinite care. This was to be his own memorial to good mates, a model of the old ship. Carving, he recalled every detail of the upper deck and below. She'd been an uncomfortable old boat, and very wet in a seaway – like a destroyer, with water slopping backwards and forwards on the roll, flooding beneath the slung hammocks, but she'd been home for a long time. . .

Hearing a step on the deck, Holloway ceased operations and looked up. A brand new officer's cap badge loomed, above a duffel-coat. Fasher. Bloody Jingo Fasher from the Pompey barracks parade ground. Holloway remembered his pal, Petty Officer Tiny Stack, now back to AB. He went on with his carving, didn't get to his feet. Sod it. When Fasher had been stamping his boots around the parade, a proper barrack stanchion, a fixture for bloody years, Holloway had been patrolling those northern waters. And officers didn't normally come into the mess-decks except for rounds and other official inspections.

Fasher said, 'What's your name?'

Holloway gave it.

'What are you doing may I ask? Skulking? That way, you'll lose your hook.'

'Off watch,' Holloway said briefly.

'Sir.'

'Sir. I could be in my hammock. But I'm not.'

21

'Watch it,' Fasher said, glowering. 'I don't like sauce. What's that you've got there?'

'Ship model, sir. My last ship . . . the *Argyll*.'

'*Argyll*, eh. Survivor? What you're doing, it's just bloody sentimentality.'

Holloway looked up, his face flushing. 'Is it, Mr Fasher?'

'Yes. And in my experience ratings usually stand when being spoken to by an officer.'

Holloway's hand clenched round the haft of the knife. He'd have liked to sink that knife in Jingo Fasher's gut and let the gas out. Instead, he said very deliberately, 'In my experience officers always remove their caps when coming into the mess-decks.'

Fasher's beefy face seemed to pale. The lips were drawn back. He said, 'There's men up there, in the hammocks.'

Holloway knew what Fasher meant. He said, 'That's right. But they're asleep. They won't be hearing anything. Not even if they're awake, maybe. You won't make anything of this – sir.'

'Let me tell you, Leading Seaman Holloway, that an officer doesn't necessarily *need* witnesses.'

Holloway smiled. 'If I were you I wouldn't put that to the test. You won't get away with it . . . not with Lieutenant-Commander Stanford you won't.'

Fasher stood for a moment like a statue, a statue that breathed hard. Then without another word he turned away and left the mess. Holloway lifted two fingers towards the retreating back and went on with his work. He felt a certain satisfaction but couldn't be unaware that he'd made a vicious enemy. Before long, Fasher would get him.

3

A SOUND-POWERED telephone whined on the bridge and Sub-Lieutenant Leyton-Seton, Officer of the Watch, took a report. 'W/T office, sir, Leading Telegraphist. Cypher from Admiralty, sir.'

'Right, thank you. Tell them to send it along to the Surgeon Lieutenant.'

'Aye, aye, sir.'

Putting back the phone on its hook Leyton-Seton debated whether or not to call the Captain and decided not to; Stanford was in urgent need of sleep and had gone to his sea-cabin only a quarter of an hour earlier. Let him stay there, Leyton-Seton thought, till the doctor had broken the signal down into plain language. The decision made, Leyton-Seton took up his binoculars and scanned the sea and the sky as he'd been doing every half-minute since taking over the watch from Hawkey. All clear. They were having luck after all; this was very unexpected. They were not so far off the North Cape now, just two more days' steaming at the convoy's speed and they should raise the cape and then come round on an easterly course between that northernmost tip of Norway and Bear Island, where the real trouble was likely to start if it didn't start sooner. According to Stanford's expectations, it should have started already. Maybe that cypher would have some bearing . . . Leyton-Seton's thoughts turned to the Surgeon Lieutenant, who, with a healthy ship's company, had damn all to do mostly except act as cypher officer and wardroom wine caterer. Leyton-Seton knew which of these lay tasks was the more congenial. Doc

23

liked dabbling about with booze, even in the abstract of the paperwork connected with the officers' wine chits. And he was pretty good. . . Father was apt to scan the monthly wine bills with an eagle eye, but Doc could be relied on to carry forward excess amounts, often making use, by prior arrangement, of the accounts of the ship's two teetotallers, Kelly and Weatherby, who were not in fact so teetotal that Father would be forced to take note. In any case, Stanford was human and knew that you had to relax in port and relaxation meant gin, and so long as – thanks to Doc's tinkering – you didn't go over the top of your own spirit tally he didn't worry.

Still both sea and sky were clear. The weather remained good, too. Flat sea, scarcely any wind. Just the never-ending cold and God knew what it would be like when they came round the North Cape, well and truly into the Arctic Circle by then.

Leyton-Seton paced the small bridge, two steps one way, two the other, passing and re-passing the binnacle and keeping an eye on the ship's course as steered by the quartermaster.

Soon the Surgeon Lieutenant came to the bridge.

'Hullo there, Doc. What's brewing in the minds of Their Lordships?'

The doctor handed him the signal form on which he'd transcribed the Admiralty message. It was short. Leyton-Seton read it without expression. He looked up at the doctor and said, 'Would you like to call the Captain and show him it yourself, Doc?'

Stanford believed in keeping his ship's company fully informed whenever possible. He used the tannoy again. 'The orders have been altered. We're to enter Murmansk instead of Archangel – a slightly shorter run as you know. I'm ordered to detach from the convoy when we reach a position due north of Murmansk, and proceed inwards independently.' He paused. 'But in the meantime, I shall be lying off the SS *Clan MacAndrew* to embark our passengers. Just for your general information, in case you're any of you interested, the *MacAndrew*'s an old ship of mine. I'd like to see some first-class seamanship. I know I'll get it. That's all.'

He switched off. He met the eyes of Leyton-Seton and the doctor, and of Hawkey who'd now come to the bridge. He said, grinning, 'I never told you, did I, I don't know why.'

Hawkey fancied he knew; Stanford was a reserved man who didn't talk about himself and perhaps he wouldn't have wanted anyone to think he might direct the defensive efforts of *Sprinter* specifically towards one particular ship – the same sort of reasoning, in a way, as that of the Admiralty in not having revealed earlier the name of the ship that was carrying the two VIPs. And the same sort of reasoning that, as Hawkey knew, took a liner officer out of his ship if any of his own family booked a passage aboard – no favouritism in an emergency. The wonder was, why Stanford had revealed it now; the answer was probably in the simple fact that he didn't want any cock-ups.

The Captain went on, 'No doubt we'll be told the reason for this shift of plan, but at the moment I'm in the dark. Number One, you'd better prepare accommodation. One of our passengers can have my after cabin, the other I'll leave to you to sort out. Someone may have to bunk down in the wardroom.'

Hawkey nodded; the 'someone' would be Midshipman Kelly, and all other officers would be shifted as it were down the line to admit the second VIP to his, Hawkey's cabin. He swung round as Petty Officer Bremner, Chief Boastswain's Mate, came up to the bridge and saluted the Captain.

'Ah, Bremner –'

'Yessir!'

'I'm still waiting for orders from the Commodore.' The Admiralty signal had been repeated to the Commodore of the convoy and to the Senior Officer of the escort. 'But I expect to lie off *Clan MacAndrew*'s starboard side for the transfer. You'd better have everything ready – port to starboard, I need hardly say, since I don't intend to back up!'

Bremner grinned. 'No, sir. I'll see to it at once, sir.'

'Thank you, Buffer.' As Bremner clattered down the ladder, the Captain turned to look towards the Commodore's ship, one of the fast RFA oilers, the *Black Ranger*. As he looked, her signal lamp began winking a message, which was read off by the yeoman of signals.

'From Commodore, sir. You may embark passengers from *Clan MacAndrew*'s starboard side as soon as you are ready.'

'Thank you, Yeoman. Acknowledge.'

'Aye, aye, sir.'

Stanford passed the helm orders to take the *Sprinter* up towards the *Clan MacAndrew*. Below on the upper deck, Bremner stood by to lower the seaboat; already the gripes had been cast off and the davits swung out. The crew stood ready to embark and pull away for the merchant ship. As *Sprinter* made her approach, a lamp was seen to be calling from the Senior Officer of the escort. The yeoman took the signal down on his pad and reported.

'From Senior Officer, sir. Admiralty reports intelligence received, German heavy units believed eastwards of Bear Island with submarines and aircraft on stand-by from north Norwegian airfields.'

Breath hissed out from between Stanford's teeth. 'We couldn't expect roses all the way,' he said, 'but it looks as though we now have the reason why the VIPs are coming across. They'll be safer – always assuming we detach for Murmansk in time!'

'And without being spotted,' Hawkey said.

Sprinter came up and lay off the *Clan MacAndrew*. The seaboat was lowered and slipped with Cameron embarked to pay the proper respects to the VIPs. The boat was pulled across smartly and fast. No one relished lying with engines stopped. Stanford had his glasses lifted on the *Clan MacAndrew*'s bridge. The list of convoy had already told him the Master's name: one he had sailed under years before as second officer. He used the loud hailer and called across.

'Hail and farewell, sir! I was with you in the *Campbell*.'

A hand was waved. 'I know,' a deep-throated voice called

back through a megaphone. 'Stanford . . . I saw the name in the list of escorts. Good luck to you, and a safe arrival. You appreciate the importance, I'm sure.'

'I do, sir.'

Stanford watched the seaboat's progress. Cameron was handling it well. The *Clan MacAndrew*'s accommodation ladder had been lowered ready, and as the seaboat made up to the foot and the crew tossed oars to come alongside, two duffel-coated figures, unidentifiable as yet, began moving down the steps. Within two minutes they had been embarked and, saluted away by the ship's Chief Officer, the seaboat came round and headed back for the falls. The moment the boat was hooked on, Stanford ordered the engines to slow ahead and gave a final wave towards the *Clan MacAndrew*.

Ten minutes later Stanford was dead.

The attack had developed with vicious suddenness just as Stanford had put his engines ahead. A destroyer on the convoy's starboard beam signalled that her Asdics had picked up a contact and she was investigating. As the destroyer heeled over under full helm and increased speed, the counter-attack orders came from Captain(D). The Commodore of the convoy began signalling: the merchant ships scattered while the escorts hurried towards the contact.

It was already too late.

As *Sprinter* moved ahead, coming clear of the *Clan MacAndrew*, the torpedo-trails were seen speeding for the heart of the convoy. Cameron, supervising the griping-in of the seaboat, was blown off his feet as a torpedo, passing slap under the frigate's counter, took the bow of the *Clan MacAndrew*. There was a massive explosion that hurled metal far and wide: lethal fragments flew across the frigate's deck and across her bridge, slivers that jagged like express-speed knives into men's bodies. Along the upper deck three seamen fell, their blood bringing more than an appearance of rust to the cold grey metal of the guns and the bitts: severed arteries had a remarkable spurt. On the bridge Leyton-Seton was still on watch, Cameron having not yet taken up his

27

action station: he looked with some surprise at blood running down his right arm to his hand, trickling from beneath the sleeve of his duffel coat. Then he saw the Captain stagger and clutch at the guardrail for support before falling in a heap.

Leyton-Seton asked the standard foolish question. 'Are you all right, sir?' He didn't catch the answer; it was no more than a mutter through lips already frothed with blood. But afterwards, trying to recollect, he believed Stanford had told him not to bother about him but to watch the ship. The first thing he did was to yell down the voice-pipe, urgently, asking for the Surgeon Lieutenant to come to the bridge. By the time the doctor arrived, Stanford was dead. The doctor didn't think there could have been much left of his lungs. Away behind the frigate now, the *Clan MacAndrew* was wallowing, well down by the head and looking as if she were about to sink. Probably, Leyton-Seton thought, her fore collision bulkhead had gone.

Below on the quarterdeck, Cameron had picked himself up: no damage. His first concern now was for the VIP passengers. *Sprinter* turned to join in the attack on the U-boat and the deck heeled sharply. Cameron saw the two passengers, clinging tightly to the handrail running around the after screen. He went across to them.

'You'd better get inside,' he said without ceremony. He opened the door in the after screen and bundled them through, then went at the double to the bridge. The Captain was still there, huddled on the deck. In his place Hawkey stood, conning the ship towards the contact. The Asdic was pinging hard. Cameron caught Leyton-Seton's eye, questioningly.

Leyton-Seton said, 'Captain's bought it.'

'I'm sorry.'

'So are we all. Are you taking over the watch?'

Cameron nodded. 'Hand over, then get to your own station.'

There was a faint, rather sick-looking grin on Leyton-Seton's face. He'd seen death before on earlier convoy runs, but never so close as this. He said, 'You sound like Number One already, Cameron.'

'What?'

'That's what you are now. Better get used to the idea.'

It was something of a shock. No time to think about it now, though. As *Sprinter* went ahead at her maximum speed, the depth-charge patterns from the destroyers were already punching up through the sea, huge waterspouts that with luck would soon show traces of oil fuel. They did.

Cameron was looking through his binoculars and reported that tell-tale streak of oil to Hawkey. Without looking round, Hawkey said, 'Not conclusive, is it?'

'No.' Often enough the U-boat captains would release a little oil to make it look as though their hidden craft had suffered damge, hoping to fool the attackers into drawing off. But within seconds something more positive was seen: long, black-painted bows broke surface, pointing up at an angle. The cheering started from the attacking destroyers, harsh and savage, triumphant, vengeful, an ugly sound but a natural one. The U-boats were the dirtier end of Hitler's war; they hadn't shrunk from sinking the liner *Athenia* with women and children aboard, and there had been more such diabolical sinkings since.

Hawkey said, 'Here the buggers come.'

Cameron saw men coming to the surface. A few moments later the bows slid back and the vessel vanished like the retreat of a killer whale. The Germans remained, waving. Shouts came across.

'Do we pick them up?' Cameron asked.

Hawkey gave a hard laugh. 'For preference, no. But we'll wait for Captain(D).'

Cameron, despite his question, knew what the answer was, what it had to be. There were other U-boats in the vicinity: already another of the merchantmen had been hit – a ship laden with machine parts, on the port beam of the convoy. Captain(D) began signalling. The yeoman reported, 'Resume station for attack, sir.'

Hawkey said, 'Port fifteen.'

Cameron passed the order down. As the ships of the escort turned away the Germans were still waving, but their shouts had diminished.

Kelly, Midshipman RNR, was at his action station, which was the after steering position in the tiller flat, a smelly place, close, dank and oily. From there you saw no action but you heard it and felt it as the guns crashed out from above and the depth charges exploded to bring the thud of drums to the steel hulls of the nearby ships. It was claustrophobic and it was dangerous: in a ship in action, greater safety lay on the upper deck, unless you were unlucky like the Captain. Kelly had heard what had happened to the Captain, that all-powerful being whom he would never have even thought of as Stanford. Now the Captain was dead, the breath ripped from his body by German action. It affected Midshipman Kelly badly: it scared him. He'd not been conscious of fear before during action, though when it was over fear had come to him in the form of nightmares in which he saw himself coming very close to violent death. Now the Captain was dead it was all different, all worse.

Captains didn't die. He knew inside himself it was stupid, but there it was: if they did die then the stuffing, the guts, was knocked out of the ship.

'You all right, sir?'

The voice itself startled Kelly for a moment, then he gave a shaky grin. It was Leading Seaman Holloway who'd spoken, Holloway who would take over the helm in secondary steering if required. Kelly said, 'Yes, why?'

'You just looked a bit off,' Holloway said, rubbing his lean face, the face the missus always said looked like a corpse, as though he didn't eat enough. It was a reflection on her, she said, to which he answered that was bollocks since he spent most of his time serving afloat. He thought about young Kelly, who looked like a sick cow. Holloway was what passed in the Navy for middle-aged – he was thirty-five – and the youngster looked as though he needed a sea-daddy. Or would have, if he'd been on the lower deck. Officers didn't have

30

such things, of course, but that didn't mean they didn't need them. Holloway grinned to himself suddenly as he reflected that the oldest officer aboard was that Fasher, and to imagine Fasher as anyone's kindly mentor was stretching it more than somewhat. As a chief gunner's mate, Mr Fasher had broken more aspiring young leading seamen than Holloway had had hot dinners. It had been said that Fasher had been eased out of 'Whaley because he never gave any young gunnery rate a recommend. They'd told him his standards were too high, but what they'd meant was that he was a nasty vindictive old bastard. Scratching at stubbly cheeks Holloway addressed the midshipman again. Young Kelly, he looked as though he was missing his rattle.

Holloway said, 'Stinky old hole, isn't it?'

'The tiller flat?'

'That's right. Don't let it get you down.' Holloway sounded cheerful. 'There's worse places. Like the engine-room and boiler-room. I don't envy that lot, sod me if I do.'

'Warmer!' The tiller flat was icy.

'Ah, warmer, yes. Too bloody 'ot if a projy gets in. All them steam pipes, flay the skin off a Pompey 'ore. You want to count your blessings, sir.' Holloway sounded sage, a real old shellback offering advice. He had to keep the kid's mind off things. He went on, 'You thought o' specializing, Mr Kelly? Gunnery like, or torpedoes, or –'

'Navigation, if the war lasts that long.'

'Ah yes, that'd be your line. That and salt-'orse seaman-ship. If you don't mind me saying so, you're a good 'and at that.'

Kelly looked pleased; praise from Holloway was worth having. What the leading seaman didn't know about seaman-ship would – if Holloway had used his own words in self praise, which was something he wouldn't indulge in – have left room to spare on a popsie's left tit. Well, that was something he was good at, Kelly thought gratefully, even though he wasn't cut out to be sealed up in a tin can like the tiller flat. Outside, the noises, which had fallen away for a while all except for the thrash and thunder of the screws right

31

beneath them – the rudder-head, by which they would steer directly if the bridge was put out of action, thrust right through into the tiller flat – those other noises had now started again. *Sprinter* was attacking. The ship laid over to full helm and a gigantic explosion came, seemingly from right slap alongside, and Kelly and Holloway were sent lurching from the bulkhead amidst a shower of paint flakings and dislodged cork insulation.

'Lord love us,' Holloway said. 'Feels like we've bloody come back over one of our own charges! You know what I reckon, sir? I reckon we'll 'ave sprung a plate or two and we'd best stand by for leaks.'

Kelly nodded. Now there was something to do, something concrete. He kept a sharp watch for tell-tale trickles of seawater. He could cope with that, knew the orders to give for the plates to be shored up. But there were no leaks and soon the noises faded away again. Kelly and Holloway lit cigarettes. Holloway screwed up the flesh around his eyes; he had something to ask and he asked it. 'Those two VIP blokes that come aboard, sir. Know 'oo they are, do you?'

Kelly shook his head. 'Not a clue.'

'No buzzes like?'

'No.'

'Bit of a mystery,' Holloway said. 'That Russian.' He ruminated. 'Bloody communist aboard a British warship, the King'd drown in 'is five inches o' bathwater if 'e knew. I reckon there's something odd going on and it means bloody trouble for us.' He added, 'Anything out o' bloody routine always does.'

Kelly was about to offer some comment when the voice-pipe whined. Holloway said, with lugubrious humour, 'I reckon that'll be for us, sir.'

Kelly answered. 'Tiller flat.'

'Bridge. The action appears to be over. Number One – the Captain – thinks there were just the two, chancing their arm. We got them both.' It was Cameron's voice.

'Secure action stations, then?' Kelly asked.

'No, Mid. We're staying closed up for dusk action stations.

All right down there?'

Kelly said, 'Yes, sir.'

This time it was Hawkey who spoke on the tannoy to the ship's company, largely for the benefit of the troglodytes below decks who had seen nothing of the action. 'You'll all know, I expect, that the Captain has been killed. I've taken over the command.' The voice held no emotion whatever. Facts were facts and the war went on, like the convoy. 'The attack's over for now. The destroyers sank two U-boats but the convoy's lost three ships. We're not, repeat not, going to lose any more if we can help it. That is all.'

Hawkey turned away from the tannoy. For a while he stood looking out over the reduced convoy, at the shepherding destroyers and frigates, at the *Belfast* wearing the Rear-Admiral's flag. It was an impressive array in the fading light with the streaming White Ensigns plus the blue and red of the RFA oilers and the merchantmen respectively; the convoy covered something over five square miles of hostile sea – a pretty big target. The sudden responsibility of command as part of the defence was big, too. Hawkey turned away from the spectacle and looked fore and aft along the decks, *his* decks now. His guns, his Asdics, his depth charges, his engines to handle to the best advantage when another attack came as come it surely would.

He turned to Cameron, standing silent and expectant behind the binnacle. 'We'll have to reshuffle the Watch and Quarter Bill, Number One,' he said. 'Your job.'

'Yes, sir.'

'Soon as dusk action stations secure. Before we're in action again – right?'

'Aye, aye, sir.'

Hawkey rubbed at his eyes. 'No alteration in routine. The Captain ran a good ship, no need for me to change his ways. His Standing Orders remain and will be re-circulated and initialled by all officers as read. See to that in the morning, please, Number One.'

'Aye, aye, sir.' The dusk deepened, though it would not be

wholly dark right through the northern night. There was always a loom of light over the sea. When the ship was sent to second degree of readiness Cameron, relieved by Weatherby, went below. Then he remembered something and went back to the bridge.

'Captain, sir –'

'Yes, what is it?'

'The passengers, sir. You'll be seeing them, I take it?'

'In the morning Number One. Make them comfortable in the meantime.'

Cameron went below again. First things first: however important, passengers were passengers and the ship couldn't wait on them. Cameron sent a messenger for the coxswain, mentioning the Watch and Quarter Bill. Chief Petty Officer Murdoch came along with the gunner's mate and the buffer. Cameron, human enough, couldn't quell the thrill when the coxswain knocked and said formally, 'First Lieutenant, sir. Watch and Quarter Bill, sir.'

Cameron would never have believed it was so complicated a task. Beside the Captain, just five men had been killed or so severely wounded that they would perform no more duties aboard *Sprinter*; but it seemed that virtually everything pertaining to the seaman branch had to be altered, the whole jig-saw done all over again. Each man in the ship had his action station, and so far as the seamen were concerned due consideration had to be given to non-substantive rates with the proper proportion allotted to each gun; similar considerations applied to second and third degrees of readiness – a two-watch system or cruising stations in three watches. A proper balance had to be maintained between the port and starboard watches, the first and second parts of each of those watches, and at the same time between the red, white and blue watches into which the ship's company was divided at cruising stations. In addition there were fire parties, damage control parties, seaboat's crew and lowerers for each watch, messengers, wheelhouse staff including quartermasters, boatswain's mates and telegraphsmen for communication with the engine-room. It was a minor nightmare of pencil-work, rubbers, crossings-out, and chain smoking.

Not until it had all been chivvied into order did Cameron make his way to the wardroom to attend upon the VIPs.

The cabinet minister was acidly displeased: he should have been introduced to the Captain as soon as action had ceased. He said as much. Cameron apologized. 'Safety of the ship, sir –'

'Yes, yes, I understand that, of course I do, but I could have gone to the bridge I would have thought. It's given a poor impression to Marshal – er.' Cameron was to become accustomed to hearing the Russian referred to by the minister as nothing but 'Marshal er'. The cabinet minister was, to him anyway, equally anonymous until, later on, Leyton-Seton told him the man's name was Harcourt Prynn and that he was the Minister for War Production. When Prynn had stated his complaint, Cameron turned to the Russian.

'My Captain's apologies, sir. He has been busy.'

'Yes, yes. I am not disturbed, not very.' The Russian was a huge man – the British minister was small and sour looking. The Russian seemed amiable, with a wide grin and a red-veined face that said it would be happy enough with a supply of vodka and never mind the Captain. There was no vodka, but gin had already been provided by Leyton-Seton for both the guests, being put down to the mess account. Cameron had the idea Leyton-Seton had been doing some arse-crawling: he already knew that the sub-lieutenant was angling for entry to the Foreign Office after the war was over. Cameron, as the mess steward came over and hovered with his cloth and tray, ordered further gin, though not for himself.

The Russian was formal. He gave a small bow and said, raising his glass, 'A toast. Their Majesty the King. And Comrade Churchill. A *good* comrade. Useful.'

The toast was drunk. Cameron proposed another. 'To Generalissimo Stalin.'

'And to Marshal Timoshenko, who is my brother-in-law.'

'A very brave man,' Cameron said awkwardly, feeling

foolish though sincere. Formal toasts were not his line.

The Marshal said, 'To marry my sister, yes.'

It could have been a joke, it could have been poor English. For safety's sake, Cameron treated it as the latter. There was some small talk; they were all keeping off the real subject, the reason for the VIPs' presence aboard. The Marshal's stomach rumbled. The cabinet minster looked much put out when he started again about the Captain and Cameron told him that Hawkey would see him in the morning.

'Not before then?'

'Not before then,' Cameron said firmly. Night was the time of danger: there would be more U-boats on the prowl, and there was no knowing whether the German heavy units, the battleships and cruisers, might decide to attack before the convoy came round the North Cape. The Captain would probably not leave the bridge all night, especially as he was new to command.

4

LIEUTENANT-COMMANDER Stanford had in fact recognized some failure of eyesight on Hawkey's part, not much it was true, but it was noticeable. He'd said nothing about it; Hawkey was RN and the Navy had to be his career. If the vision got worse, then Stanford would have spoken to him, but for the time being he hadn't had the heart. He, the Captain, was the one who had at all costs to see and never fail to see; and he'd made a point of being on the bridge when Hawkey was on watch – this trip, that was; the defect hadn't been noticeable to Stanford till after *Sprinter* had cleared away from Loch Ewe at the start of the current escort duty. Captains usually took the chance to get some sleep when their second-in-command had the bridge watch, so Hawkey had guessed that the Captain knew – he was well enough aware that Stanford had confidence in his abilities, thus there had to be some other reason.

Motionless in the fore part of the bridge as *Sprinter* kept protective station on the convoy, Hawkey took stock. He could be hazarding many lives; yet as Captain the lookouts and the Officer of the Watch were his extra eyes whilst on the bridge. Seamanship, general upper deck work, anchoring, securing alongside, making up to a buoy – if a humble frigate should ever be accorded a buoy – all these were important too. He could have caused an accident by not seeing something he should have done when lowering a boat, for instance; some piece of careless seamanship could have passed his eyes by. It didn't matter so much now he had assumed command; he had a First Lieutenant to see to all that

37

kind of thing. But if it got worse, then he would have to report it and get Doc to make him an appointment ashore, if ever they landed up in a port where there was an eye specialist handy. Next time they were in for a boiler clean, perhaps. It could improve but he doubted it. It had been coming on so slowly to start with, then it had suddenly worsened, and there was a dull pain somewhere behind his eyes most of the time.

The binoculars hurt his eyes but they had to be used. As ever in time of war all the ships were steaming without lights and although the loom on the water gave some vision those great dark shadows could change their outlines with quite astonishing speed when one of them got out of station and mucked up the others. Merchant service officers were not all of them familiar as yet with the exigencies of station-keeping. The Commodore was all right aboard his RFA – the fleet oiler officers were accustomed to sailing with the battle squadrons in peacetime, and the ships themselves had the engines to cope with the delicate 'up four revs, down four revs' needed to keep dead in station relative to the next ahead and on either beam.

Tonight, for some reason – probably perversity, Hawkey thought with a grin, since he was facing his first night in command – the ships were all over the show and the Commodore was busy trying to shepherd them back into line. Captain(D) was weaving dangerously in and out of the convoy lanes, appearing now and again at risk of having his stern sheered off as he came close round a big, bluff bow.

'Captain, sir.'

Just for a moment Hawkey didn't think he was being addressed; then he turned. The visitor was Mr Quince, Warrant Engineer – the Chief, as he was customarily known.

'Hullo, Chief. What can I do for you?'

'A spot of trouble brewing up, sir, below.'

'God! It would be! Go on Chief. Don't say it's condenseritis again.'

'Basically, yes, sir. With complications.'

'Can you cope?'

'Oh, we'll cope all right,' Mr Quince said, sounding slightly offended. 'It's not that. It's that I may have to –'

'Stop engines? I'd got that far. Bugger! When?'

'Within the next couple of hours or so at the most, sir. Not for long – I hope.'

'So do I, but I don't need to itemize the dangers to you, Chief. *How* long?'

Quince shrugged; he'd come up in his overalls, which were thin, and he was shivering. 'Hard to say for sure, sir. I never like to make promises what I can't keep to . . . but I'd say an hour'll see it through.'

Hawkey nodded. 'All right. No time like the present.' He swung round. 'Yeoman, make to Senior Officer repeated Commodore, Regret must stop engines for about one hour.'

'Aye, aye, sir.' The yeoman of signals went to the rear end of the bridge and started calling with his blue-shaded Aldis. It was often necessary to make signals at night but they could be a giveaway to a lurking U-boat, one not yet within range of the Asdics; Hawkey found his nerves playing him up as he waited for the answer to his signal. God damn condenseritis, a plague that tended to afflict ships that had spent long periods thrashing around the seas. Engines and boilers, over-used, played up; seawater got where it should never be and the condensers, the chambers that condensed the steam as it left the cylinders, didn't like it. For most of the time it could be lived with but now and again something had to be done to alleviate the sickness and now was one of those times.

The answer came from the Senior Officer of the escort: *Quick as you can. Catch up when ready. Good luck.*

Hawkey shrugged himself deeper into his duffel-coat. The cold was worse than ever. The latest weather report brought to him by the Petty Officer Telegraphist indicated that conditions ahead were even colder, that snow squalls could be expected once they were into the Barents Sea . . . but by that time they wouldn't have far to go. If they were lucky.

He said, 'Stop engines, Number One.'

'Stop engines, sir.' Cameron passed the order down.

Hawkey said, 'Remember the signal, Chief. Quick as you can.'

39

'You bet,' Quince said with feeling, and went fast down the ladder to the upper deck. He didn't need telling to be quick; he'd be like greased lightning so far as speed was consistent with doing a proper job. If he had to improvise, then he would improvise: he was well accustomed to doing that. HM ships seemed always to be short of spares these days even though the factories were working at full pressure to keep them supplied. And often enough there were cock-ups in the dockyards, the wrong parts being put aboard, wrong parts that had been known to slip past his scrutiny, a very mortifying thing to happen to a Warrant Engineer. Mr Quince went through the air-lock into his engine-room, small and neat and with a worried expression. The Chief Engine-Room Artificer was on the starting platform, a piece of cotton-waste in his hand. The ship wallowed; the silence had an uneasy feel, was broken by little other than the slop of the sea against the thin side plating.

'All right, sir?'

Mr Quince nodded. 'Skipper's a bit jittery, Ted. Can't say I blame him.' He repeated Hawkey's adjuration. 'Fast as you can, eh.'

Ted Dunlop, Chief ERA and Number Two in the engine-room, nodded and left the starting platform, automatically wiping at shining metal with his cotton-waste. The skipper wasn't the only one who was jittery: Quincey was and all. Bag of nerves and over-conscientious with it. Drive himself round the bend if he wasn't careful. Dunlop happened to know one of the reasons for his Engineer Officer's anxious state of mind: Mrs Quince. Quincey and Dunlop were old friends and had done three commissions together pre-war, up the Straits, China-side and the Home Fleet back in the days when it had been called the Atlantic Fleet. And both lived in Pompey within a stone's throw of one another. Like that tower of bombast, Fasher, Quince had only fairly recently got his warrant, but that was the only point of similarity. Quince and Fasher were poles apart, and why that Fasher's wife, if he had one, stuck to him, God alone knew. Perhaps she hadn't, come to think of it. Poor old

40

Quincey's hadn't: she'd gone off with a bloody Jack Dusty, a Supply PO from *Vernon*, the torpedo school at Pompey. That had left Harry Quince with just the one thing: his professional competence. He was a dedicated engineer and as straight as a die. If ever he slipped, and that wasn't often, he crucified himself afterwards but never passed the buck, never cast blame. Dunlop knew he wasn't of the same stamp, that he would never make a warrant officer. He'd got as far as he was going: he wasn't so dedicated. He went now, slow and solid and big-bodied with a humorous face, to sort things out. Quince went with him, leaving a junior ERA on the starting platform.

The monotonous slop of the sea jagged at Quince's nerves.

The convoy moved away, heading east-nor'-east at its fourteen knots. *Sprinter*, although she had around six knots' speed in hand if she was both lucky and pushed really hard, was going to be stretched to overtake if she lay stopped for much more than the hoped-for hour. Hawkey wondered about his passengers: they hadn't been mentioned in the exchange of signals, so clearly the Senior Officer was relying on that one hour's estimate as being a reasonably accurate forecast. Hawkey was avid for a cigarette – you couldn't smoke on the bridge or the upper deck at night, for some prowling U-boat captain might see the strike of match or lighter through his periscope. The lookouts to port and starboard watched closely, sweeping their binoculars through their arcs as their fingers froze beneath the woollen gloves produced for their comfort by knitting bees throughout the UK. Gloves, balaclavas, scarves . . . the good ladies of the Home Front made them all, and though Hawkey couldn't for the life of him have said what a 'bee' meant, he thanked God for its existence. He thought of his mother: she didn't knit or sew, never had, but she was serving in a forces' canteen at a Scottish base, none of the troops or naval ratings or airmen knowing that her husband was Vice-Admiral Sir Rufus Hawkey, retired from the Navy two years earlier and recalled to serve as a commodore of convoys such as this one. Lady

Hawkey, who had but the one son left – Hawkey's brother Johnnie had been lost early in the war, serving as a sub-lieutenant aboard the aircraft-carrier *Courageous*, sunk by U-29 not far off the entrance to the Bristol Channel – was a substitute mother to many serving men. She wrote letters home for those who were illiterate – they didn't mind confessing that to her – she relayed messages to girl friends when the young men had sudden draft orders or their ships went unexpectedly to sea, and she listened sympathetically to opened hearts when bad news came out of the blue from homes in the areas strafed by Hitler's bombers.

And she had every possible faith in her surviving son, whom she saw, peering into the future far beyond her own life span, hoisting his flag as an Admiral in command of a battle fleet.

James Hawkey hadn't wanted to go to sea. But since he hadn't known just what he wanted to do, his future had been decided for him: RN Special Entry after leaving Haileybury. He often wondered why he hadn't been sent to Dartmouth at thirteen and a half; his own wishes had never seemed to matter very much to his father. He didn't even now realize that that had been due to his mother: she knew he hadn't wanted it and she fought for him. But in the end, at seventeen and a half, his father had won the day. And then, after Johnnie's death in action, so gloriously, his mother had begun to see him, James, as the future carrier of the Hawkey flag. A mantle had descended upon him. He had never had the heart to tell her how much he hated it all. He wondered, sometimes, if she knew. One thing he was sure of: he'd managed to conceal his feelings from everyone he'd served with. His pride wouldn't have allowed him to do less. And his pride saw to it that he hadn't made anything of his eyesight problem; it would have seemed, at any rate to himself, like an excuse, a let-out.

Now the convoy had all but gone: just a few distant smudges, patches of greater dark, scarcely seen at all unless you had the advantage of knowing they were there.

Hawkey wished the time away. To feel the throb of the

42

main engines under his feet would be balm. There was a lonely, left-behind atmosphere, a nasty feeling of desertion. *Sprinter* was only a frigate; as such no one would be unduly disturbed about her loss. The convoy would survive. That was inherent in the mere fact that the Senior Officer, comfortable aboard the *Belfast*, had not left a destroyer behind to stand by and act as guard. *Sprinter* wasn't worth a further depletion of the convoy's defence – and fair enough, Hawkey thought, shrugging. That was the way of things; but there was still the question of those passengers. He was surprised that they hadn't aroused concern before the escort and convoy had disappeared ahead – but only a little surprised. However important, they absolutely could not be allowed to alter a whole convoy pattern and deprive the merchant ships of more of their defence capability – in this war, material had become incomparably more important than any man – while to start a re-shuffle to another ship held its dangers. And the fact that *Sprinter* was not a highly valuable vessel as compared with others could of itself explain why they'd been chosen to take over and eventually land the passengers; Hitler would expect them to be accorded a bigger and more splendid ship.

Think of the devil . . . there was a step on the bridge ladder and Hawkey heard a voice, not Hitler's, addressing Cameron. 'Lieutenant, is that your Captain?'

Before Cameron could answer, Hawkey did so without turning his head. 'I am the Captain, yes. And you?'

'My name is Harcourt Prynn.'

Hawkey, who had guessed as much from the authoritative yet at the same time petulant voice, nodded. He said, 'I intended meeting you tomorrow forenoon, sir.'

'A long time ahead.' Harcourt Prynn sounded disagreeable.

'I'm sorry. I have my ship to worry about.' Hawkey wished he hadn't used the word worry; captains shouldn't worry. They should decide and command. But Harcourt Prynn probably wouldn't get the nuance anyway. 'However, now you're here, sir. . .' He turned and reached out a hand.

Harcourt Prynn shook it limply. 'How d'you do, Captain. I

43

believe I've met your father. He was Fourth Sea Lord before the war, was he not?'

'Yes, sir.'

'I thought so.' Harcourt Prynn hesitated. 'I decided to come up here because I was concerned about the fact we were stopped. Indeed I was woken up by the cessation of sound and a different motion.'

'I'm very sorry about that, sir.'

'I trust there's nothing wrong?'

For a moment Hawkey almost boiled over. He wanted to say, to shout, No you bloody old idiot, of course there's nothing wrong, we often stop engines in the middle of the hogwash and let the convoy bugger off without us, it's a nightly occurrence, didn't anyone ever tell you? Instead he said, 'Nothing that won't be put right soon.'

'Well, I must say I'm glad to hear it. It's not very reassuring, to find one has stopped. You do realize how *vital* it is that we reach Russia – soon and safely? I shall be meeting Marshal Stalin himself if all goes well. I shall be representing Mr Churchill and the War Cabinet, you know. This is really sickening, Captain.'

'What is, sir?'

'Why, this delay. It doesn't seem very efficient. I suppose you have a capable engineer.'

'Very capable.'

Harcourt Prynn blew out his cheeks; in the faint loom of light from the binnacle he looked like a barrel of lard, soft and flabby. Hawkey boiled again and this time he failed to contain the steam.

He said politely, 'I understand you're the Minister for War Production, sir?'

'Yes, yes, that's quite right. Yes. Mr Churchill –'

'Let's forget Mr Churchill for a moment, shall we? Let's concentrate on War Production. It's a bloody pity you don't do that more often!'

'Do what?'

'Concentrate on your job. My warrant engineer's hamstrung by lack of parts, by constant frustration every time we

44

enter a naval dockyard, by turned-down requests for this, that and the other, by constantly deferred refits – because not enough war production's being achieved. And that's one reason why you're stuck here tonight, Mr Prynn. As Minister for War Production I'd say you were a dead loss.'

Harcourt Prynn gave a gasping sound followed by a snort. Then he turned and went down the ladder.

There was a silence on the bridge; the lookouts went on looking out, the yeoman became very busy checking his flag locker. Hawkey said, 'I shouldn't have blown off steam, Number One. What?'

'No, sir.'

'Made an enemy, haven't I?'

'I expect so.'

Hawkey laughed. 'Never mind. I feel a damn sight better!'

It had started as condenseritis but it had ended as something very much worse. A steam valve had jammed up solid and a ham-fisted leading stoker, by name Pinnock, in attempting to free it with a clamp on the controlling wheel, had broken the fitting off. It was, said the stokers, typical of Pinnock. Scalding steam had escaped and by the time the Chief ERA had plugged it, the engine-room was filled with mist. Mr Quince called the bridge to report.

Hawkey asked, 'Any casualties, Chief?'

'No, sir, by a bloody miracle. But for now we've had it.'

'How d'you mean?'

Quince said, 'I mean I've got a temporary plug on the leak and to get it there I had to shut off steam. If I opened up again, the plug wouldn't take it.'

'And the net result, or have I guessed it?'

The warrant engineer grinned mirthlessly into the sound-powered telephone. 'I reckon you have, sir. I can't put steam on the main engines till I've fitted a new valve, and I haven't got a new valve. For that you can blame the bloody dockyard.'

Hawkey swore, staring out across the cold, empty sea. 'Can you make one, Chief?'

45

'I reckon so, yes, but it'll not be a fast job. Having said that, I'll be as quick as I can.'

'I know you will, Chief.'

Quince put back the receiver and wiped sweat from his face. He nodded at the Chief ERA. 'Take over, Ted. I'm going to see to this myself.' He left the starting-platform and went up the spider's-web of steel ladders to the air-lock and out into the alleyway, making for the engineers' workshop. In there, they were already working on the new fitting and they didn't need Quince to chivvy them. They all knew the score. They all knew the culprit, Leading Stoker Pinnock, as well; Pinnock was equally well known on the seamen's messdeck. Pinnock played, when the exigencies of the war allowed, for the ship's football team. A few weeks ago *Sprinter* had beaten an eleven from the mighty *Nelson*, and this victory had been ascribed to the perspicacity of the Sports Officer, Midshipman Kelly, in giving Pinnock *carte blanche* to annihilate the enemy. When becoming the subject of a tackle by Leading Stoker Pinnock, the men from the *Nelson* had been all but murdered. It had taken the spirit out of the team very effectively. All honour to Pinnock for that; but as dawn came up and *Sprinter* still lay silent, heaving restlessly, Pinnock was the target of a number of mostly acrimonious conversations to do with his engine-room antics.

'Bull in a bleedin' china shop,' Holloway said. 'All brute strength and no brains, that's Pinnock. Cack-'anded's not the word. Jesus! I s'pose I'm prepared to die for the King if I 'ave to, but not for bloody Pinnock.'

Now it was dawn action stations. After making rounds of his guns, Fasher climbed to the bridge. Hawkey was huddled where Stanford used to huddle: he hadn't left the bridge all night and there were dark shadows under his eyes. Every now and again he rubbed at them, hard. Hearing Fasher's approach, he turned.

'Morning, Guns.'

'Good morning, sir. This is a pretty kettle of fish.'

'Yes, isn't it.'

Fasher's eyebrows went up a fraction. The skipper had sounded funny, sort of reprimanding almost, or anyway off-putting. Fasher wasn't going to be put down like that. He said, 'Engine-room ratings putting the ship at risk isn't my idea of the way to fight a war. I've heard what happened. Me, I'd strip that Pinnock of his hook.'

'I'm sure the Chief can cope, Guns.'

'Well, I hope so, I'm sure.' Fasher stared around. There was heavy cloud forming to the north: that looked like snow. He said, 'We're going to be in the muck soon, all right. Why don't they get a move on below I'd like to know?'

Hawkey didn't think the remark worth responding to; he was using his binoculars again and the pain was worrying him. Both sea and sky were clear of everything but that cloud-bank, which was extending south towards them, extending fast. When it struck, the visibility would come down to nil. Well, at least that would provide cover.

Hawkey lowered his binoculars and rubbed once more at his eyes. For a moment Fasher seemed to dance before him and to be rimmed in a red light like a bull-shaped neon tube, then the gunner resumed his normal stability. As he did so he asked, 'How much longer, eh?'

'I don't know,' Hawkey said.

'Chase 'em up below, sir, will you?'

'No. They're doing their best, Guns. No point in being a damn nuisance. They don't like sitting around here like a duck any more than we do.'

Fasher shrugged. 'Well, it's up to you, of course, but I always believe in a charge of dynamite being applied – works wonders!'

'On the parade at Portsmouth?'

Fasher stared, seemed about to offer some edgy retort, then thought better of it. The skipper was the skipper and as for himself he was a very new warrant officer; but not being entirely insensitive he was beginning to hoist in a certain sardonic attitude on the part of all hands towards his hitherto cushioned war and he wanted to hit back. You couldn't hit back at the skipper, but the skipper wasn't the whole ship. His face angry and truculent, Mr Fasher turned to leave the bridge. As he set foot on the ladder the first snow flurry hit them, and the visibility, already coming down fast, closed right in. But not before a report had reached the Captain from two sources: the radar, and the starboard bridge lookout.

It was the human eye that reported first. 'Ship bearing green four-five, sir!'

Hawkey swung his binoculars up: he caught the merest glimpse of a dark blur on the horizon before all visibility went and the vessel was lost. It was then that the radar cabinet called the bridge. Hawkey said, 'Do better next time. The bridge lookout beat you to it.' He turned to the ordinary seaman concerned. 'Well done,' he said briefly. 'Number One, the ship will remain at action stations until we see what happens next.'

'Aye, aye, sir,' Cameron answered.

Fasher had come back from the ladder now. What d'you think it is, sir?' he asked.

Hawkey shrugged. 'Could be anything – friend or foe, merchantman or warship. I didn't get a good enough look.' He called to the lookout. 'What's your estimate, Bonner?'

'I can't say, sir. All I saw was something that looked like it might be a ship, sir.'

Hawkey, already powdered like the others with the falling snow, called the engine-room. 'Chief, Captain here. There's a vessel in the vicinity and no visibility left. How's it going your end?'

'Not too good, sir. I'm sorry. We've just tried out the fitting and the thread's stripped. I was just going to report. I'll put something together, never fear.'

Words rose in Hawkey's throat, an urgent need to bawl someone out and relieve his own pressure. But he held on to himself: the Chief was doing his best, they all were, and temper didn't help. He said evenly, 'All right, Chief, just carry on. I'll keep you informed as to what goes on up top.'

'Very good, sir.'

Hawkey banged the sound-powered telephone back on its

48

hook and turned to find Fasher staring at him and looking dour. Fasher's face said quite clearly that it was a Captain's job to give abuse in some circumstances and this was one of them. Hawkey met the gunner's stare. He said, 'You came up here for a purpose, I expect, Guns, apart from commenting on the engines. What was it?'

Fasher said, 'Before that ship was sighted, that was. Committal of the dead, that's what, sir –'

'While we're stopped?'

'Engines is always stopped when the dead go overboard, sir.'

'Yes, I know that. But not when –'

'When you can't move away afterwards. I take the point, sir. But the sea's pretty disturbed and I reckon they'll go easy. And it's not a good thing to keep bodies aboard. There's such a thing as morale.'

Hawkey said, 'Later, Guns.'

'But look –'

'For Christ's sake, Guns, not now!' Hawkey turned his back. Fasher gave an angry snort, said, 'It was you who asked,' and clattered down the ladder to the upper deck. Hawkey's mouth was set in a hard, thin line. His eyes were hurting again, the snow as it fell on the exposed bridge and the gun-shields and the links of the cable seemed to have a reddish dye, like the blood that might cover his decks if that unknown ship should blunder into them in the murk. No one could say whether or not the frigate had been spotted from the other ship; but if she was a warship it was likely that she would be equipped with radar. Just then the next report came from the radar cabinet.

'Bridge, sir. Vessel closing, still bearing green four-five, sir.'

'Thank you.' That ship could be homing on to them by radar, and it was a virtual certainty that if she was alone she would be a warship – even the neutrals were using the convoy system now. If she wasn't alone, the radar would have picked up other contacts. Whatever it was, it spelled out extreme danger to a frigate wallowing without power on her main

49

engines. Hawkey, with Cameron and the lookouts, stared uselessly through his binoculars, trying in vain to penetrate the heavy snowfall. Soon the ship was covered and had lost its outline. Along the upper deck the buffer could be seen, moving like a white shadow as he set the hands to work with brooms, clearing away the snow before it could freeze on the guns and decks and rigging to bring a dangerous top-weight that in extreme cases could capsize a ship.

5

THERE was a silence throughout most of the ship, above and below; even the scrape of the brooms was hushed by the snow. The tension was immense as they all waited for something to happen. Cameron made his way round the ship, checking on the damage-control readiness. Men were tending to speak in low voices, as though the invisible vessel might pick up sound. It was an eerie feeling and it affected the ship's company in different ways. Only in the engine-room and in the radar cabinet was there normality. And the radar, a thing of dials and knobs, green streaks and brilliant moving blobs, something of a mystery still to all but its dedicated practitioners, indicated that the unknown ship was coming in still on a closing course.

Cameron went back to the bridge. Hawkey stood like a snowman, white from head to foot. Despite the buffer's efforts, the snow was piled thickly on the fo'c'sle, the deck gear looming like hummocks in a winter field. The cold was intense, penetrating the layers of warm clothing.

Hawkey said, 'I'm thinking about sound signals, Number One. Vessels not in sight of each other.'

'Two prolonged blasts, sir?'

Hawkey said, 'Yes.' That would indicate that his ship was technically under way but was stopped with no way upon her. 'I think we should do it when she gets closer. The radar plot shows her heading right for us and I see no point in being sunk by collision.'

'Won't she have radar, sir?'

'We don't know, do we?'

51

'We don't want to give ourselves away unnecessarily.'

Hawkey said, 'Look. If she maintains her present course, she's going to hit. Then she'll know we're here, all right! Check with the Chief that he's still got steam on the syren, Number One.'

Cameron called the engine-room. Mr Quince reported in the affirmative; steam, however, was still not available to turn the main engines. Hawkey passed the word via Cameron that all hands not immediately required in the engine-room and boiler-rooms were to come up on deck and that the Chief was to stand by to evacuate the rest at short notice. Quince passed the word to his Chief ERA and as a number of the hands went up the ladders he turned back to the job in hand, feeling a wateriness in his guts. All his working life had been spent in the engine-rooms of warships, from battleships and cruisers and destroyers down to this perisher . . . good places to work in but not to die in. You could never evacuate fast enough – you couldn't get too many men out through the air-lock at one time – and he would be, by duty and his own conscience, the last to leave. And if the ship's plates should be fractured by any impact of hull or projectile, the engine spaces would fill within minutes – seconds if the fracture was big enough. They would all be floated to the deckhead and held fast there to drown as the cold sea pressed in. Mr Quince had a curiously strong premonition that he wasn't going to come through this trip, that even if they didn't get sliced in half within the next few minutes then the bloody Jerries were going to get him before he was back inside the boom at Scapa. Well, it was an ill wind . . . that Supply PO at *Vernon* might find some balm, no need to go through all the muck-raking of a divorce. So would Nessie and good luck to her. Quince thought about his wife. Married eighteen years: he'd been an ERA third class then, marrying on a pittance a girl he'd first seen behind a bar in Devonport. He'd transferred her to Pompey and a two up two down in a road off Arundel Street. No children; but from what the neighbours used to hint at when he got back from foreign commissions, that hadn't been for want of trying on Nessie's part. The wonder was, she hadn't flown the nest years ago.

Quince turned as he felt a hand on his shoulder. He met the eye of his Chief ERA.

'All right, John?'

'Yes, Ted.'

The grip tightened. 'Doesn't do to brood. Forget it. It's the only way.'

'Don't be bloody daft.'

Ted Dunlop grinned, but the grin was a hard one and if he'd had that Supply PO handy he'd have smashed his teeth in. Dunlop had been Quince's best man even though he'd taken the liberty at the time of warning Ted off the Devonport barmaid. He knew just how Quince felt now. But Quince was fighting it down and his mind was back on the job. He leaned across one of the ERAs working on the valve.

'Give it here, Lacey,' he said. 'You're as cack-handed as that Pinnock, lad.'

The minutes ticked past. The invisible vessel was still holding her course, according to the continual reports coming through from the radar operator. On the bridge Cameron felt his hands grip the binoculars like a vice as he stared towards the bearing, waiting for the moment when a hull would materialize out of the falling snow – but by then it would be too late. The visibility was down now to no more than twenty or thirty yards. When the radar reported the oncoming ship to be fifteen hundred yards off the starboard beam and closing still, Hawkey reached his decision and passed the order to make the standard sound signal.

Two prolonged blasts from the steam syren blared out, a deep-throated roar that ripped through the crowding snow-flakes, a rude intrusion of sound into the silence enveloping the wallowing frigate. When the shatter of noise died away Hawkey and Cameron listened intently with the rest of the bridge personnel.

'No response,' Hawkey said. As he spoke, the next report came through from the radar cabinet. The other ship hadn't altered. The range was down to twelve hundred yards now.

53

Hawkey said, 'She's going to ram, Number One.'

'Do we abandon, sir?'

'Use your loaf, Number One! No, we don't abandon, not unless we want to freeze to death. This is the Arctic Circle, not the Med. When I was in the Ark –' He broke off. The telephone from the engine-room was whining at him. He snatched the thing up. 'Captain here. Clear the engine spaces, Chief. You've got just minutes.'

'One moment, sir.' Quince's voice was hoarse, almost cracking. 'We're almost there. I'll have steam back on –'

'Too late, Chief. Get 'em up and get 'em up pronto.' Hawkey slammed the cover back and swung round on Cameron. 'Nothing more we can do now. Except pray if you feel inclined.' He turned to face towards the oncoming ship, the ship that even now could not be seen. Cameron believed he was in fact praying as the cold snow layered his right cheek with flakes that froze as they touched the skin. Cameron himself found a prayer coming into his mind and he said the words beneath his breath and with sincerity. Beside him the yeoman of signals, a widower, thought of his two children and his mother who looked after them: this was the sort of ultimate thing he'd joined for and there was no denying that, but it would be the innocent who would suffer when he went, not that there was anything unique about it. He felt like jumping overboard and ending it quick, but discipline held and he just stood and waited by his signalling projector and sucked his teeth and hoped for a miracle. His old man had been in the last lot, in the army, a maimed survivor of Mons . . . suddenly, he gave a hard laugh and Cameron turned.

'What's the joke, Yeoman?'

'No joke really, sir. I was just thinking of the Angel of Mons. Too much bloody snow and thick weather for one to show up here.'

So Cameron was thinking of angels and that strange manifestation seen by many thousands of troops in the sky over the blood and misery of a battlefield in Belgium, when the awaited ship appeared suddenly from the blinding snowfall.

54

They were all out of the engine-room and boiler-rooms now, all clustered on deck where at least they might have a better chance.

All except Mr Quince and the Chief ERA. Quince had said, 'The job's nearly done and I can manage on my own. Get out, Ted. Skipper's orders. Mine, too.'

'Bollocks to that,' was all the Chief ERA said, and lent a hand. He was wet with sweat and his fingers felt like putty, fumbling and useless. He kept telling himself, more haste less speed. He wasn't stopping to reflect that whether or not that valve was made to work it was certainly too late. He didn't waste time thinking that a ship wasn't like a car that could get away straight from stop. He just got on with the job, him and Quincey, mates like they'd always been and still were even though Quincey now wore an officer's cap-badge.

As they worked with single-minded purpose, extraneous sounds came to them. A sound like subterranean thunder, with a regular beat to it.

'Screws,' Quince said briefly. He stopped work for a second, eyes staring unseeingly across the engine-room, his spotless, shining kingdom. What it might look like soon . . . he got back to it again, capable hands moving with careful efficiency. The beat of the churning screws grew louder, drumming through the frigate's steel plates. Christ, what a war. Somehow it had never occurred to Quince, not back in the days of peace, that they might be required to fight in the waters of the far north, right round into the Barents Sea. He had never seen Russia as the gallant ally of the King of England and Winston Churchill; it was unnatural. All those Bolsheviks, for whom in a sense he was currently working. The peacetime Navy had been accustomed to thinking in terms of the Med and the Far East, plus the West Indies . . . such places as Gibraltar and Malta, Alexandria where the Med Fleet had shifted to from Malta during the Abyssinian lash-up when Musso had attacked the Lion of Judah, Emperor Haile Selassie, and Musso's general, known as Electric Whiskers, had started off by being beaten by the fuzzy-wuzzies . . . Colombo, Singapore, Hong Kong, Shanghai and Wei-hai-Wei, Bermuda, Cape Town. Not this lot, this freeze-up under skies of lead. This wasn't the Empire. Mr Quince didn't think much of Stalin's ideas.

The job was okay now. Quince nodded at the Chief ERA, who slid the handwheel into place, gleaming brass. It locked on. Quince wiped sweat from his eyes and felt a shake throughout his whole body, a reaction setting in, a reaction that made his legs feel wobbly and useless. He said, 'Thanks, Ted.'

He was on his way to the starting platform to report to the bridge when the deck lifted beneath him, suddenly and staggeringly, and then dropped back again. Seconds later there came a fearful racket from for'ard, a harsh grinding of metal, of tortured, fractured steel, and the engine-room lurched and heaved and then seemed to spin in circles.

Cameron had seen the great, grey loom first and had given a shout of warning. The stem of what looked like a battle-cruiser rose above the frigate's bridge, pushing a wall of sea ahead of itself. It was this that had lifted the frigate and flung Mr Quince back from the starting platform below.

Then she had hit, slicing through the frigate's fore section, cutting like a knife through butter, and moving on to drag the full length of her massive armoured sides across the screaming, torn metal where the seas now washed full against the collision bulkhead. The men on *Sprinter*'s bridge saw the German ship's company looking down upon them, grinning, shouting, waving fists, saw the snow-covered stream of the Nazi ensign, dimly, at the peak. Then she was gone, her wake tumbling against the frigate's shattered bows.

Hawkey, his face grey against the snow's white, stared for'ard. He said, 'It looked like the *Scharnhorst* or the *Gneisenau*. Thank God the convoy's gone ahead. Better sound round, Number One. I'll want a report on the collision bulkhead.'

'Aye, aye, sir.'

As Cameron left the bridge, the report came in from the

engine-room. 'Steam on the main engines, sir.'

Hawkey let out a long breath. 'Bloody well done, Chief! Thank you. We're in trouble for'ard but we may be lucky. I'll keep you informed. Meanwhile, I'll be sending your hands below as soon as I have the reports from damage control.' He paused, then asked, 'By the way, do I take it you disobeyed orders and stayed below, Chief?'

'Aye,' Quince said. 'That's about it, sir.'

Up top, Hawkey grinned. 'All I can say is, much obliged!' He replaced the voice-pipe cover and turned to Leyton-Seton who had taken over the bridge watch when dawn action stations had been piped earlier. He said, 'I don't believe she'll come back. Those Nazis'll think they did us in. And for all we know yet, perhaps they have.'

Leyton-Seton nodded. 'I'm surprised they didn't open fire, sir.'

'Don't be, I'm not. No need to waste ammunition in the circumstances, was there?'

'I suppose not.' Leyton-Seton swung his arms about his body. God, it was cold. Real brass-monkey weather. To have gone into the drink would have been colder and by this time he would have been a corpse, swirling down to the bottom before eventually rising again bloated with gas and starting to decompose outwardly as well. Leyton-Seton shivered at his own thoughts. Eton hadn't quite prepared him for this sort of thing and never mind the bullshit about Waterloo and the playing fields. True, Eton had had its heroes in battle and he'd heard plenty about those patriotic *ex alumni*, but it was different when death had stared you in the face, breathed on you, and passed by – till the next time, and the time after that, war without end, amen. His thoughts turned elsewhere fairly quickly: his stomach felt empty. He asked, 'How about breakfast, sir?'

'*Breakfast?*' Hawkey turned and stared. 'Christ above, Leyton-Seton, first things first if you don't bloody well mind! The hands'll be piped to breakfast just as soon as it's possible and that won't be yet. I suppose you do realize there'll be casualties down there?' He swept an arm towards the fo'c'sle.

57

Leyton-Seton might have looked red-faced had he not been almost obliterated by the snow. 'Yes. Sorry.'

Hawkey grunted and turned his back. He was congealing inside, or felt that way. How anyone could think about breakfast was beyond him. He could visualize the fo'c'sle well enough if Leyton-Seton couldn't.

Cameron had a first-hand sight of the messdeck beneath the fo'c'sle and it sickened him to retching point. He had to pass through, with the buffer and the shipwright, to make his inspection of the collision bulkhead, which in fact was holding, though sprung in many places. It would need to be plugged and strengthened with shoring beams. It had been set back a little at its top and some of the starboard side plating had been stove in for some considerable distance, fortunately above the waterline, and fractured so that a slop of sea was entering on the roll. That, too, would have to be worked on but he reckoned the ship was still seaworthy. A gale would bring difficulties, but currently there was no gale, just the snow which seemed never to end. And it wasn't the structural damage that was affecting him. One of the damage control parties had been stationed in the seamen's messdeck and three of the men had been nipped by the sudden staving-in of the side plates while another, who must have been flung into the air by the impact, had been caught around the neck by the topside of the collision bulkhead as it was pushed inward, after which, by the shipwright's guess, it had eased back a little, just enough to catch the man's neck between it and the deckhead above. The head itself had been crushed and the neck severed; the body had dropped to the deck and was lying in a slop of water. Blood was everywhere. The bodies nipped into the curl of the side plating had burst. There was no other word for it. The pressure had sent the blood out like a series of fountains and it was still dripping from the deckhead and the opposite side of the ship.

Cameron didn't feel like breakfast either.

He didn't say a word to the buffer. Petty Officer Bremner knew what had to be done without prompting. Having passed

58

the orders for making the fore part of the ship seaworthy, Cameron carried out an inspection throughout the frigate, ensuring that no other plates had been sprung and no vital parts subjected to any potentially dangerous strain.

Then he went back to the bridge to report.

He saluted the Captain. 'Not too bad, sir. We're not making any water except in the seamen's messdeck and we'll cope with that.'

'Casualties?'

Cameron gave Hawkey the facts and Hawkey, looking screwed-up and sick, said, 'Oh, sod the war, Number One. Sod Hitler!'

'Yes, sir.'

'I take it, in your opinion, we can steam?'

'Yes, sir,' Cameron said, then added, 'Not just my opinion, sir. The buffer and the shipwright too.'

'Learn to trust your own judgment, Cameron. It's your report I asked for.'

'Yes, sir,' Cameron said again. 'As a matter of fact, the full weight of the sea's being kept off the bulkhead – to some extent it's cushioned. A length of the starboard side plating is sort of wrapped around. It's acting as a shield. Of course, it'll probably affect the steering a bit.'

'The whole bloody business'll affect the steering, my dear chap!' In an almost routine movement, Hawkey brought up his binoculars and examined the euphemism for a horizon all around. The snow was thinning now but that horizon was still shut right in, maybe half a mile, which was some improvement at least and a good thing it hadn't come earlier or the German would have seen them still afloat. As it was the Jerry was still moving away on his original course, more or less, according to the radar. Hawkey had a sudden thought, one he should have had earlier. He said, 'The bastards'll still be getting echoes off us, presumably. They'll know we haven't gone down, if that's the case. Since we have steam again, we'll lose no more time.' He moved to the sound-powered telephone but was stopped by Cameron.

Cameron asked, 'With sternway, sir?'

59

'Won't the collision bulkhead take headway, is that what you're saying?'

'It'd be safer not, sir. Just in case.'

'Safer,' Hawkey repeated, rubbing at his eyes. 'This bloody war isn't about safety, Number One, it's about chances. We'll have a better chance going ahead, since we can steam a damn sight faster that way. What you'll have to do is watch that bulkhead like a vulture, that's all.' He called up the engine-room. 'Captain. I'm rejoining the convoy. Engines to slow ahead, just to see how she takes it. All right, Chief?'

'All right, sir. My hands —'

'Coming down now.' Hawkey spoke to Leyton-Seton without turning. 'Pipe the engine-room complement to return below, Leyton-Seton.'

'Aye, aye, sir.' Leyton-Seton passed the order to the wheelhouse and a moment later the boatswain's call shrilled out along the upper deck. Within the next four minutes the frigate was once again and at long last under way, thrusting the icy seas from her shattered bows.

Hawkey said, 'Well, thank God that's over. Now you can have your wish, Leyton-Seton.'

Leyton-Seton seemed puzzled. 'Sir?'

'Hands to breakfast,' Hawkey said sardonically. 'And secure from dawn action stations.'

Sub-Lieutenant Weatherby came up to take over as Officer of the Watch and Leyton-Seton went below to wash and shave. By the time he reached the wardroom breakfast was ready. It was the best the officers' steward could raise from the galley but it wasn't much. Frigates at sea were not the Savoy, not even a temperance hotel for commercial travellers in a provincial town, as Leyton-Seton remarked with a sigh to Mr Fasher: they were faced with corned beef in all its naked glory, with tea. Leyton-Seton elaborated on temperance hotels for commercial travellers; he'd stayed a night in one once, by sheer force of circumstances, when passing through Cardiff. Everything else had been full and the hour was late and he'd been more than a little tight. On waking to a hangover in the morning, he had been faced with a religious text on the wall opposite his pillow. It hadn't done him much good, he said lightly. And the breakfast was better forgotten; but it hadn't been as bad as this.

'Be thankful to eat at all,' Fasher said, sounding surly.

'Oh, I am, I am, never fear, Mr Fasher. This just happens to be putrid, that's all.'

'Tastes all right to me.' The gunner lifted his plate and sniffed. 'Smells all right, too.'

'I didn't mean it literally, Guns. Just a figure of speech, don't you know.'

'No, I don't know, Mr Leyton-Seton. Perhaps it was a bit above my head. Perhaps my education was lacking.'

'Oh, come now, Guns, don't say that. Where were you at school?'

Fasher said rather over-loudly, 'Albert Road Elementary, Pompey. You?'

'Well, actually, Eton.'

Fasher gave a snort and conversation languished. A moment later the increased throb throughout the ship indicated that Hawkey was putting the speed up, and that must mean the collision bulkhead was holding.

The clearing of the remaining snow, as the frigate began to leave the heavy squall behind at last, was proceeding aft on the quarterdeck under the direction of Leading Seaman Holloway and being only slightly impeded by the slow and desultory movements of Able Seaman Dander, known, on account of his three good conduct badges, as Stripey. Stripey Dander, a man of thirty-eight who looked fifty, was a perennial grouser even though he was a good seaman, or would have been if he'd forced himself to hurry more on occasions. He was a lifelong martyr to indigestion, and hurry made it worse, or so he said. He was accustomed whenever possible to plague the life out of the doctor and the sick bay. This morning he was aggrieved because the leading sick-berth attendant, being busy, had told him to fuck off. Stripey knew there had been casualties but the living had their rights as well and there was no need to be rude.

61

And now that Holloway was chasing him.

'Come on, Stripey, keep the circulation going.'

'Bollocks.'

'The cold's bad for indigestion, remember.'

Stripey groaned and pushed harder with his squeegee, which, with not much snow left, was more effective than the brooms. He said, 'Talk about chokka. I'm up to here.' He lifted a hand, demonstratively, to his chin.

'What about, this time, eh?'

'Bloody convoys. Those poor sods who've bought it. All for the bloody Russians.'

'They're under pressure, Stripey. Bloody Adolf –'

'He can press all 'e bloody likes, Killick, sod me if I care.' Stripey Dander took the opportunity to lean upon the shaft of his squeegee. All rest was welcome and Holloway never seemed to mind a natter, he was a good bloke really, not all push and shove and get fell in, like some. Maybe Holloway had had enough of the war too . . . a different kettle of fish from that Fasher who gave every sign of thriving on it, no doubt hoping to turn his warrant into a commission by stepping into dead men's shoes. Stripey elaborated on his theme: it would be a bloody sight better, he said, if bloody Hitler had been allowed to get at bloody Stalin's throat so they could both be finished off together without any British dying in the cause of Bolshevism. Neither he nor Holloway had noticed a thickset, bulky figure in a duffel coat and balaclava who had emerged from the door in the after screen and was standing watching them.

'Shower o' buggers,' Stripey went on loudly. 'Murderers an' all. That Stalin thinks 'e's God. I'd give 'im a piece o' my mind if I could get me 'ands on 'im. Look at all the ships we've gorn and lost, and what do we get out of it, eh, you tell me that, Killick.'

The duffel-coated figure advanced and thrust four-square between Holloway and Able Seaman Dander. 'I tell you,' he said in a hard voice. '*I* tell you, not him.'

'Oh, yes? And 'oo are you when you're at home, may I ask?' Dander felt Holloway's seaboot come down hard on his toes, but it was too late.

'I am Marshal Yurigin.'

'Oh.' Stripey looked abashed.

Holloway saluted and said, 'Very sorry, sir, I'm sure. It wasn't intended.'

'Yes, it was intended. But you do not know so cannot be blamed. Your leaders, all capitalists, keep you misinformed with lies, wicked lies, you understand? You are fed with opium, wool is pulled. When the war is over, you will perhaps be taught the truth. Your Churchill is useful to Russia now, but he is a capitalist, and soon his day will be over, and the sooner the better.'

'You leave Mr Churchill alone,' Holloway said. He was getting heated. Churchill meant something special to the Navy: First Lord in the last lot, First Lord again at the start of this one. Holloway remembered the signal that had gone out to the Fleet when the old man had resumed office: *Winnie's back*. Every ship's company had cheered when they heard that. That and his V-sign, which endeared him further to seamen's hearts because they knew that *he* knew very well what they equated it with – it seemed to bring the common touch. Winnie was the man who would eventually see Adolf Hitler stuffed. Not the Russians with all their OGPU, all their Siberias and Kremlins – they were the soul mates of Hitler, really.

Holloway, not a man to mince words, said as much. That was a mistake. Marshal Yurigin lost his temper and seized Holloway by an arm. Holloway was shaking it off, roughly, when Fasher looked down from the splinter screen aft of the gun platform.

6

Fasher was down to the quarterdeck like greased lightning. He shouldered Holloway aside and saluted Marshal Yurigin smartly, a real Whale Island tear-off. 'I apologize on behalf of the Royal Navy, sir. May I ask what happened, sir?'

Yurigin snapped, 'The man was rude. That is all.'

'And attempted to strike you.'

'Bollocks I did,' Holloway said.

'I wasn't asking you. I saw what happened. I asked the Marshal for confirmation.' Fasher addressed the Russian again. 'He attempted to strike you, sir. I –'

'No. I think he did not do that.' Marshal Yurigin was summing Fasher up fast, not that much effort was called for to spot a bully. Fasher wore the cap-badge of an officer above his duffel coat, and all the world knew of the undemocratic way of life in the Royal Navy, knew of the terrible power of the officers against the seamen. That it was similar in Russia was of no consequence. A good communist, when abroad as now he was, did not add to the sufferings of the proletariat. It had been the Russian Fleet that had acted as the precursor of the revolution: Marshal Yurigin remembered the great mutiny at the Black Sea port of Odessa some thirty-six years earlier, years before the overthrow of the Czar. The officers had been seized and asked the question: Do you like it hot, or do you like it cold? If the answer was cold, fire-bars were secured to their feet and they were thrown into the icy waters to drown. Those who liked it hot were fed live into the furnaces by the sweating stokers. The Czar's retaliation had

64

been ferocious. Marshal Yurigin said. 'The man did not strike me.'

Fasher rose and fell on the balls of his feet, hands clasped behind his back. The Russian, like all Russians, was a bloody liar. Fasher didn't like the Russians or the need to keep them supplied any more than Holloway did, but Holloway was his victim and he was going to get him. He said, 'I see. Then I shall have to accept that. But he *laid hands* on you. I know he did, since I saw him with my own eyes, sir.'

'Yes. This he did. But I had laid hands on him –'

'I didn't see that, sir, and it's not important.' Fasher called out to Stripey Dander. 'You there, that man.'

'Yessir!'

'Fetch the cox'n. At the double. Move!' Stripey lumbered off for'ard. Fasher turned again to the Marshal. 'If you'll just leave it to me, sir. It's a matter of ship's discipline. I'd take it kindly if you'd return to the wardroom whilst the charge is made out.'

Speaking to a marshal or no, there was something formidable about Mr Fasher, Gunner RN. He had terrified many a parade ground; he didn't exactly terrify Marshal Yurigin, but he had made his point and Yurigin didn't propose to lower the dignity of the USSR by arguing. He shrugged and turned away and went back into the superstructure, where in any case it was a little warmer. Fasher, with an ugly smile twisting his lips, looked at Holloway.

'Now then, Mister bloody Leading Seaman Holloway,' he said.

Holloway stared back at him, thinking of his friend Petty Officer Tiny Stack as was, sweating it out as an AB again thanks to Fasher. In a low voice he said, 'You're a bastard, Fasher, a right bloody bastard. And there's no one round to hear me tell you so.'

'Like the other day in the messdeck, right?'

Holloway said, 'Right.'

The smile was still on Fasher's face. He said, 'Let me refresh your memory, son. You said –'

'*You* said an officer didn't need witnesses. Yes, I remem-

65

ber.'

'And you said, that wouldn't wash with Lieutenant Commander Stanford. Well, Lieutenant-Commander Stanford's dead. Now we have Hawkey.' Fasher stepped back a pace as the coxswain was seen coming along the deck.

Sprinter seemed to be making it well enough; a first-class job had been done on the shoring-up and plugging of the collision bulkhead and of the torn and twisted side plating and the ship was pushing into the seas at around fifteen knots. The overhauling of the convoy would take time, too much time at that speed, and Hawkey began gradually to increase it while Cameron stood by with the shipwright and a party of seamen in the fore messdeck, watching the bulkhead. Revolution by revolution the screws speeded up, and all seemed secure. Cameron made continual reports to the bridge. Then a message came down to say that the Captain was unwell and the First Lieutenant was required on the bridge.

'What's the matter with him?' Cameron asked.

'Don't know, sir. The doctor's with him,' the boatswain's mate answered.

Cameron nodded. 'All right, I'll be up. Who's on watch?'

'Mr Weatherby, sir.'

'Right. My compliments to Mr Kelly, and I'd like him to take over at the collision bulkhead.' As the boatswain's mate made his way aft, Cameron climbed to the bridge. Hawkey was still standing in the fore end, half leaning over the bridge screen, and the Surgeon Lieutenant was at his side.

Cameron asked, 'What's the trouble, Doc?'

'Exhaustion,' Surgeon Lieutenant Goode answered briefly. It was a fact that Hawkey had hardly left the bridge since before Stanford had been killed. 'It's affecting his vision, but he won't –'

Hawkey cut in. 'My vision's perfectly all right.'

'Not what you said to Weatherby,' the doctor said.

'I didn't know what I was saying. I was all in.'

Goode nodded, and winked at Cameron behind the Captain's back. 'All the more reason for you to go below. I

66

prescribe bed rest, sir. In fact, I insist on it.'

'I do the insisting, Doctor.'

'With respect, that wouldn't be wise. Look. Why keep a dog and bark yourself? What's the point of Their Lordships appointing a medical man if –'

'All right, all right. I'll do as you say. It's probably best, I suppose.' Hawkey seemed to be out on his feet; he slumped sideways and his duffel coat fell open from the toggles and Cameron saw that his polo-necked jersey was still soaked with the entry of the snow earlier. His face was grey and drawn, the skin over the cheek-bones tight and parchment-like. Goode whispered that the Captain would need assistance down the ladders, and Cameron nodded at Weatherby, who passed the word to the wheelhouse. The boatswain's mate and a messenger came up and, with the doctor in rear, Hawkey was helped towards the ladder where he stopped and turned round.

'I won't be long, Number One. Look after the ship, won't you? She's not steering too well.'

'I will, sir. Don't worry about anything.'

'You're not to hesitate to call me in accordance with Standing Orders.'

'Aye, aye, sir.'

Hawkey shambled down the ladder like an old man. After he had gone Cameron asked Weatherby what had happened. Weatherby, his round face cheerful still, said, 'He just seemed to collapse, so I sent down for Doc. I think it's what Doc said, just exhaustion.' He sounded confident of his diagnosis.

Cameron grinned. 'Goode'll be glad of the confirmation. How about this business of vision?'

Weatherby was puzzled about that. He said, 'Well, that was funny. Just before he collapsed – perhaps that's too strong a word really, he just sort of staggered a bit – just before that he said he couldn't see a bloody thing, everything was red and distorted. Then he seemed to recover. He was using his binoculars and didn't say any more about it.'

Cameron nodded and brought up his own glasses for a

sweep around the horizons. The day was much improved now and there was even a hint of blue sky at intervals as the clouds scudded along before a rising wind. Cameron, glad enough of the absence of the appalling blizzard, wasn't too happy about the wind. That could cut their speed quite a lot, seeing as it was coming from dead ahead and the collision bulkhead might not take a really heavy pounding. He felt his responsibility; until the Captain was fit, the first decisions would be his.

He was on the bridge when the coxswain came up and reported a defaulter to the Officer of the Watch.

Climbing to the bridge, Leading Seaman Holloway reflected that it had become a bloody weird sort of world. All that 'sir' to a communist, who, whether or not he was a marshal, was a bloody bolshie – a real one, not just some sea-lawyer on the messdeck who got known as having bolshie views on life. Until so recently, Russia had been the enemy, the factual ally of Hitler. Russia had swooped like a venomous vulture on little Finland and swallowed it whole. Nothing had been bad enough to say about Russia. They had to be just about the King's worst foe in all the world: kings were anathema to them. Yet now they were the King of England's mates and, judging from the papers, he didn't seem to mind. Holloway, not versed in the wiles of politicians and statesmen and their ability to become chameleons, felt thoroughly chokka. A few months ago the laying of hands on a Russian, which in fact he hadn't done, would have received a commendation, if not a medal; but now he was in the rattle because of it and if Fasher had his way he would lose his rate – like Tiny Stack. Maybe worse: he could get cells, to be served out aboard the depot ship when they returned to Scapa. Or even detention, which was much more serious and would mean Detention Quarters in Pompey or more likely Barlinnie Prison in Glasgow, which Holloway believed was currently being used by the ships in Scottish waters when they had a customer to land.

And all because of a perishing bolshie . . . or the fact that Stripey Dander had shot his mouth off in the first place. He should have sat on Stripey, hard.

Holloway went up the bridge ladder in the wake of Fasher, with the coxswain behind again. Reaching the bridge, the coxswain saluted the Officer of the Watch.

'See a defaulter, sir, please.' There was no question-mark; it was like an order. Chief Petty Officer Murdoch, senior rating in the ship, combining his duties as torpedo-coxswain with those of master-at-arms, chief of the ship's police, was a power to be reckoned with.

Weatherby said, 'Very good, cox'n,' and moved into the port wing of the bridge in order to establish the fiction that the First Lieutenant, into whose report the defaulter might go for the next stage of the judicial proceedings, could not pre-hear the case.

The coxswain rattled off the charge. 'Leading Seaman Albert Peter Holloway, sir, official number P/JX 079654. One, did at 1025 hours this day whilst in charge of a party clearing snow from the quarterdeck lay hands in a hostile fashion upon the person of Marshal Yurigin of the Russian armed forces, passenger aboard this ship. Two, did use insubordinate language to his superior officer, namely, Mr Edwin Arthur Fasher, Acting Gunner, Royal Navy, the words complained of being, You're a bastard, Fasher, a right bloody bastard.'

'Which,' Murdoch said later to the buffer, 'is just what Fasher is. This is a bloody pity, Buff. You'll agree with me that Holloway's a good hand?'

'The best, 'Swain, the very best. Anyway, what happened?'

'Well, Subby had no choice, had he? First Lieutenant's report. Mr Cameron'll have no choice either. It's a serious charge, got to go before the skipper.' Murdoch lifted his glass, containing his daily tot of rum – neat to chief and petty officers, three parts water to junior ratings – and gave a toast. 'Bloody bad luck to Fasher, Buff. I'll be seeing what can be done.'

Petty Officer Bremner gave him a shrewd look. 'Going to

69

stick your neck out, are you, 'Swain?'

'There's ways and means,' Murdoch said.

There were. In due course the coxswain went to the bridge, where he had a word in Cameron's ear. Cameron said he would speak to the Captain as soon as he could, and meanwhile he would hear nothing about it if Murdoch should pass the time of day with Marshal Yurigin. Well satisfied, the coxswain was on his way back down the ladder to the upper deck when a heavy wave took the fo'c'sle and a moment later there was a report from the seamen's messdeck.

Midshipman Kelly was not facing his first experience of watching over a shored-up bulkhead. Two years earlier, before he had joined the RNR, he had been aboard a Clan liner that had had her bows damaged by gunfire from a surfaced U-boat, after which the Master had turned and rammed, much to the surprise of the German captain. The bows had been stove right in and the water-pressure had come upon the for'ard collision bulkhead and set it back in a somewhat similar way to what he was now watching. So he knew the signs. The moment he heard an ominous cracking sound, and saw an increase in the incoming trickle of water that was being continually baled out from the deck, he knew he was in for trouble though he didn't know just how much.

He gave the orders immediately. 'Get one of the spare beams up, fast as you can, the starboard one's had it. And watch out for yourselves.'

Kelly worked with the others: it was a case of all hands and no time to spare, no shirking danger. With surprising speed and plenty of foul language the new beam was lifted and laid with one end against the bulkhead and the other footed down hard against the next bulkhead aft, well chocked down with hammer blows against the wooden wedges as the collision bulkhead began to take on a nasty convex bulge inwards. Kelly himself swarmed up the baulk of timber to chock down the fore end against the bulkhead but the job took longer than he had hoped.

The initial report to the bridge had informed Cameron that

70

one of the beams was coming under undue strain. This was followed by a second report: another beam was now in place and was holding, and yet another was being set in place as a further precaution.

And Kelly was dead.

Cameron was deeply shocked. Kelly had had his whole life before him, had been almost the youngest of the frigate's complement. He asked how it had happened. He was told that Kelly had been knocking home the wedges when an increased pressure of the sea – even though the first thing Cameron had done on getting the original report had been to stop engines – had sent the wedges flying and had finished off the starboard side beam – broken it in half very suddenly and without further warning. The vast piece of timber, its jagged ends sharply splintered, had been driven sideways into the midshipman's body and he had been virtually disembowelled. On arrival, the Surgeon Lieutenant had pronounced him dead, not that there had been any doubt about that from the start.

Cameron turned away and, staring out across the sea wastes, swore luridly for more than half a minute. Russian convoys . . . when Holloway had been brought up in front of Weatherby, he had repeated what he'd said to Marshal Yurigin, honestly and without holding back – Holloway was that sort. Cameron now agreed with every word. The Russian run had slaughtered too many good men, and Russian thanks were scarce. Was it all worthwhile? Would they, once the war was over, come to regret the waste? Kelly had been a good seaman; Holloway still was.

That afternoon, at four bells, Fasher at last had his wish as expressed earlier: the dead were committed to the sea. Hawkey insisted on getting out of his bunk to read the service. He looked half dead himself, Cameron thought as he looked down from the bridge on the pathetic scene, the canvas-shrouded bodies flopping formlessly into the restless sea, bending in the middle as they fell.

71

7

HARCOURT Prynn, Minister for War Production, didn't like communists either. He was due for a difficult time in the USSR. They were a pressing bunch and thought Britain could work miracles and by the very nature of his job and his mission he was going to be regarded as the fount of miracles. The thought depressed him; he hadn't a lot to offer. British servicemen were already going short in some of the many war theatres; yet Russia had to be sustained, Hitler had to be kept fully extended eastwards. Both Churchill and the service chiefs were adamant on this point. Nevertheless Harcourt Prynn was going to get the rough edge of the Churchillian tongue when he got back to London if in the meantime he had been inveigled into promising Stalin too much in the way of war material. That was, unless he had been able to strike a bargain. Churchill was looking ahead to the future when the fighting would be over and the world realigned itself for peace.

Harcourt Prynn disliked his travelling companion, the marshal, intensely. The man was a boor; the fact that Prynn himself was much agitated by the recent delay to the ship's progress had not been helped by the Russian's attitude. The fellow complained endlessly about British inefficiency and the fact that a person of his importance had been put aboard a vessel likely to break down. Prynn had defended the ship's officers, realizing that to some extent – as Hawkey had rudely reminded him – his own reputation was involved in the poor supply situation, the non-availability of spares. The Russian was a dyed-in-the-wool communist and had made remarks

72

about the uselessness of the capitalist system supported by Harcourt Prynn and his colleagues. He was unarguable with; he stated everything as a fact. He was, of course, a man of the people, the sort of person that Prynn – rather like Leading Seaman Holloway – failed to see in the same sort of role as someone like, for instance, Lord Gort, or Ironside, or Auchinleck or indeed any other British general. This was why he always referred to him as Marshal er. He simply couldn't bring himself to link the rank to the name.

Harcourt Prynn was aware that he was a poor choice to go to Russia and aware, too, that Churchill thought the same. But his job had dictated; no one else of his status had everything at his finger-tips and the Russians would not have accepted an underling. Sitting now in the wardroom, listening to the inconsequential chatter of Leyton-Seton and Weatherby, Harcourt Prynn grew more and more morose. He didn't fit into the scene; no one talked to him for more than a few polite exchanges before drifting off with some excuse; only the Russian, who entered the wardroom fifteen minutes later.

Yurigin sat alongside Prynn, on the leather settee running along the bulkhead below the two ports. He said, 'I spoke to you about a man who was rude this morning.'

Prynn sighed. 'Yes.'

'I have spoken to another. An important person among the men, not an officer.'

'Really.'

'Yes.' Yurigin was not keeping his voice down; the wardroom had emptied, suddenly as wardrooms do when work or the need to sleep calls. Only the steward was around, clattering dishes in his pantry. 'This man said the other man would be much punished. He spoke of the system. I do not like your system. It is the class system. All is wealth and privilege, those who are not of the officer class live as rats in squalor, in cages. The man who spoke to me was sympathetic, and is an admirer of Comrade Stalin. All is not well in your fleet. It is not for me to add to misery. I said to this man, take away the charge. I do not wish to press. He answered that this was possible only to one person – the Captain. It is to the

73

Captain that speech must be made now that the system has begun.'

Harcourt Prynn was bored; he cared nothing for naval procedures.He said, 'Then if I were you I'd go and see the Captain.'

Yurigin said firmly, 'No. Not me. You.'

'It's none of my concern.'

'I say it is. You are a minister. You shall order. I do not wish to be involved.'

Harcourt Prynn gave an impatient laugh. 'I'm in no position to give orders aboard a ship!'

Yurigin was insistent. Harcourt Prynn was to do as he said. The ship was British; for a Russian to interfere might be annoying, his motive might be misunderstood, and the British being what they were things might go worse for the man, who would be used as a vehicle for revenge. Comrade Stalin, whom Harcourt Prynn was to have the honour of meeting, would be displeased. Comrade Stalin felt deeply for the oppressed everywhere. It would be well for a British minister to show compassion.

Against doctor's orders, Hawkey was back on the bridge; he was rested now and though he still felt unwell he could not remain in his bunk. The frigate had come through the bad weather and was now steaming fast through comparatively flat seas. Darkness had come down and the cold, as they made far to the north, was intense and cruel. It went straight to a man's guts; bare steel could not be touched by unprotected flesh. Touch anything, and you left some skin behind. Spray, coming aboard over the broken bows, froze in the instant of splashing down. The fo'c'sle was a sheet of ice and once they had passed eastwards of the North Cape the whole ship was likely to be in a cocoon of it. Every step along the upper deck would hold danger. No one would move without a hand on the lifelines, rigged fore and aft along the whole extent of the deck.

By now everyone was waiting for the radar to pick up the convoy. They shouldn't be too far off; the eventual sight of

74

the merchant ships and their escort would be heartening. They had been too long alone. In these war days, one grew accustomed to sailing in company and now the sea had a naked look as it lay empty beneath the hidden lead of the skies.

Hawkey said, 'No moon, that's something to be thankful for, Number One.'

'Yes, sir.'

'Come here a moment, will you.'

Cameron stepped away from behind the binnacle, moving to the Captain's side. Hawkey spoke in a low voice. 'I had a visitor to my cabin. Our tame minister, Prynn.'

'Yes, sir?'

'To do with Holloway. He asks for the charge not to be proceeded with – Fasher's charge. As a matter of fact, that was the first I'd heard of it. I had a word with the cox'n afterwards. . . I gather Holloway's been put in my report, by you. Care to fill me in on detail?'

Cameron did so. Hawkey said, 'I understand Yurigin doesn't want it to go ahead. But if it comes before me, it'll have to. Fasher was an eye-witness. Then there's the charge of insubordination, the words used to Fasher. In the circumstances, I can't see that the two can be separated.'

Cameron blew out his cheeks. 'I don't like any of it.'

'Nor do I. It's decent of Yurigin to withdraw it. We can take it he won't offer evidence, but that may not be enough, taking into account Fasher's involvement. And Holloway's a good lad.'

'Can't you dismiss the case, sir, when it comes before you?'

Hawkey shook his head. 'Again, I refer to Mr Fasher! You can't just dismiss something that's been actually witnessed by an officer, Cameron.'

'Caution, sir?'

'Not possible, on a charge like that. There's only one way as I see it. The charge sheet has to be torn up.'

'You mean we just forget about it, sir?'

Hawkey shook his head. 'Not exactly. I'll get Fasher to withdraw. It's scarcely in accordance with the proper service

75

manner and all that, but that's what I propose to do.'

'And Fasher? What do you use to make him withdraw?'

Hawkey laughed, edgily. 'The requirements of diplomacy! I'll point out that in this case the minister's wishes are paramount and I'll even put a few words into Churchill's mouth if I have to. I'll stress that after due reflection I've decided that even the personal charge of insubordination mustn't be proceeded with or Yurigin won't be satisfied. In the meantime I'd be obliged if you'd have a private word with the cox'n – the forenoon will do, tomorrow. The point being, I don't want too many discussions on the bridge, for obvious reasons.'

Cameron said, 'I'll see to it, sir, and glad to.'

'Thanks, Number One. When you've done that I'll see Fasher in my sea-cabin.'

The whole ship was against Fasher by this time. The word had spread quickly, helped on its way by Stripey Dander who wasn't admitting to his part in upsetting Marshal Yurigin in the first place. Holloway was a popular leading hand. Fasher had already made his unpleasant mark on the ship; it wasn't, in the messdecks' opinion, up to a barrack-stanchion to chuck his weight around. Holloway wasn't in fact the only one aboard who had past experience of Fasher: there was another, a two-badge AB named Parsons who had not been present in the seamen's mess the day Holloway had brought Fasher off shore. Years before, during an earlier infliction of Fasher on the barracks, Parsons had suffered Detention Quarters as a result of Fasher's mendacious representations at the defaulters' table. Not unusually with Fasher, Parsons had been unable to prove his case. Fasher was adept at the giving of doctored evidence, the more so since on this occasion he was saving his own skin. But not so long ago now, Parsons had come into possession of the proof he'd been lacking at the time. A long while after the event, but still usable. Fasher didn't know this; Parsons had not swum much into Fasher's ken since the latter had joined *Sprinter* and in the years following their last encounter Parsons had grown a

76

luxuriant beard and had suffered a broken nose when the boom of a sailing cutter had struck him during a Fleet regatta in the Med. Also, there had been one other change, an important one . . . Parsons was pondering the chances of putting the squeeze on Fasher, wondering if the time had not come to reveal all, get his own back and assist Holloway, when his ruminations were cut short by the urgent din of the action alarm. With the rest of the off-watch men, already mostly out of their hammocks since dawn action stations had been piped, Parsons made a dash for the upper deck and his station in the wheelhouse. Way ahead of the frigate there was a U-boat, just lying on the surface, at extreme range but starkly visible beneath the clearing skies of the emergent dawn.

On the bridge Hawkey was examining the U-boat through his binoculars. 'What d'you make of it, Number One?' he asked.

Cameron shrugged. 'Mystery, sir!'

Hawkey went on looking. 'Damaged, I fancy,' he said after a while. By this time Cameron, too, had picked up the possible signs: the U-boat was a little down by the head, with the sea washing aft along the fore casing towards the conning-tower, and she was listing to port.

He said, 'Damaged in an attack on the convoy, sir?'

'Likely enough, the bastard. Looks as though he expects me to take off survivors – which is why he hasn't opened fire.'

'Are you going to?'

Hawkey said, 'No, I'm not. Not with our two passengers aboard. It could just queer some pitches, though don't ask me how – I'm just not going to take the risk.' He went to the after part of the bridge and called down, having caught sight of Fasher. 'Guns!'

Fasher looked up. 'Sir?'

'I'm going in to sink her by gunfire.'

'Aye, aye, sir!' Fasher was keen, right enough.

Hawkey turned to Weatherby, who had arrived to take over as action Officer of the Watch. 'Engines to full ahead, Weatherby, wheel five degrees to starboard.'

77

'Engines full ahead, sir, starboard five.' Weatherby repeated the order, passing it to the coxswain on the wheel below.

'Midships . . . steady. Number One, watch that bloody bulkhead like gold dust!'

'Aye, aye, sir.' Cameron went fast down the ladder, sliding the rail through his hands, feet scarcely touching the treads. As he went for'ard the frigate, under full power, began shaking throughout her plates; the wind made by her passage sighed eerily round the ropes and wires of her standing rigging. So far there was no response from the German, who might still be expecting salvation. It was dirty but it was war, and it was the Nazis who had made it dirty in the first place. On the bridge Hawkey stood watching carefully, judging his moment to make the turn that would bring all his guns to bear. He was in fact praying that the U-boat would be the first to open: that would take away some of the feeling of dirt. Seamen were seamen whatever their nationality. The Germans were only doing what they'd been ordered to do, and it was just their luck that they were in this case doing it in a submarine, which Hawkey happened to regard as one of the nastier of man's inventions.

His prayer was granted: not quite in the way he'd intended. The U-boat opened as the range closed and *Sprinter* came a little across her bow. Her gunnery was good. A shell went smack into the frigate's superstructure aft and there was a loud explosion.

'*Fire parties aft!*'

Weatherby passed the order down. Hawkey, tight-lipped now, said, 'Starboard ten. Midships. Steady! Open fire.'

The U-boat was now smack on their port beam. The frigate's main armament opened from fore and aft, emitting gunsmoke and ear-splitting crashes. Weatherby had stuffed his fingers into his ears and still felt deafened. The fall of shot was not too brilliant, both projectiles falling short of the target and sending up spouts of water that momentarily obliterated the U-boat. Frenzied shouting could be heard from Fasher. Then there was a whistling sound and a rush of

78

air as a shell sped over the bridge. This time, the German gunnery wasn't quite so hot. Hawkey, as *Sprinter* went on past the U-boat, ordered port helm to bring his guns to bear again; and once more they crashed out. Now the ranging was better: a flash appeared on the U-boat's after casing and the submarine jerked and reeled in the water.

Hawkey called out, 'Well done!' The next salvo took the conning tower at its base, blowing a gaping hole in the plates. Faces were seen, and a good deal of blood spilled from bodies lying across the after rail. Hawkey took his ship in closer; at the close-range weapons a gunnery rate took aim and pumped away while spent cartridge-cases rained to the deck around him. The Oerlikons swept the casing and the conning tower; men went down like ninepins. One more shell came across and went right through the frigate's funnel without exploding. Soon after this the close-range weapons had despatched the German gun's crew.

Hawkey said, 'Cease firing.'

The guns fell silent. There was an eerie silence, soon broken by screams and cries from the Germans that were left alive. Very suddenly, the U-boat rolled over and sank. There was a vortex in the water and a lot of hissing steam, plus oil fuel and bits and pieces of men's lives – smashed woodwork, articles of clothing, fragments of paper, together with bodies belched up through the broken plates. Hawkey felt a sense of awe and horror that his word had done all that. Victory when it came could have a sour note. He became aware of a thick-set man climbing the bridge ladder: Marshal Yurigin, with congratulations.

'You have done well, Captain. Such a result is pleasing. Comrade Stalin will like to hear of this.'

'Thank you,' Hawkey said. 'I'm so glad.' He thought: stuff Comrade Stalin.

Cameron came up to report. The bulkhead had held but the pressure resulting from the high speed of the attack hadn't done it any good. More strengthening was necessary.

A little later that morning, something else didn't do him, personally, any good either. When he went as asked by the

Captain to talk in private to the coxswain, he happened to be seen by Fasher. Soon after this, Fasher was sent for by the Captain and told in no uncertain terms that the charges against Holloway had been dropped and he would have to co-operate. Hawkey came out with a load of what Fasher thought was sheer bull about the Russian and the over-riding demands of diplomacy and the war situation overall, the trust between allies and a lot of tommy-rot like that. Fasher knew that was all eyewash, and did his own putting together of two and two. That Cameron: he'd been along to natter at the coxswain. Cameron's face had shown on the bridge that he didn't like the charge. He'd twisted the skipper's arm – Hawkey, in Fasher's view, was as soft as soap, a let-down for the RN. As for that Cameron, he was typical of a half-hard RNVR. Civilian ideas didn't fit aboard a warship. Cameron hadn't the guts to maintain discipline.

So in future he'd better watch it, because he, Fasher, was going to get him.

The cabin accommodation below the upper deck had suffered little damage but the wardroom had been burned out when the shell had entered the after superstructure; the explosion had left little more than a spatter of flesh from those who had been in the compartment, closed up at their action stations. Among them had been Goode, the Surgeon Lieutenant, and his LSBA. In action, the wardroom became the medical dressing station.

The Minister for War Production, together with Marshal Yurigin, was safe though shaken. When the alarm rattlers had sounded, Harcourt Prynn had got out of his bunk and, wrapped in a thick dressing-gown and his overcoat, had emerged on to the upper deck: he had had a feeling that it was safer to be out in the open during action. He suffered from a degree of claustrophobia at the best of times. When the shell entered the wardroom he was standing just below the bridge superstructure on the starboard side; there was a safer feeling when you couldn't actually see the enemy. Harcourt Prynn thought of the House of Commons, the ultimate authority that sanctioned the building of ships like *Sprinter* and sent the armies into the field of battle. The House could itself be a kind of battlefield and Prynn had fought in his time; indeed, the struggle had been long. It wasn't easy for a man without influence to make his way in the Conservative Party and come out close to the top.

Prynn had entered parliament young: the 1922 General Election, the parliament under the leadership of Bonar Law that had lasted a mere eleven months and twenty-seven days, after which Prynn had gone again to the hustings and was returned to serve under Stanley Baldwin. He had lost his seat in the first of the two 1924 elections but had been returned again for a different constituency in the landslide of 1931 when the National Government had been formed. He had stayed there in 1935 and soon after the election had become PPS to the Minister of Transport, his foot then on the first rung of the ladder. What he preferred not to think of as toadying had brought him advancement, if slowly and painstakingly. Then there had been some fortunate deaths, and he had risen further. Largely, it had been a case of being in the right place at the right time.

Like now. Harcourt Prynn shuddered to think what would have happened had his footsteps taken him towards the wardroom. Relief that he was alive swept through him and was succeeded by anger that he should have been exposed to such danger. He was a VIP, of value to the war effort, the lynch-pin of the mission to Moscow, and when the frigate had developed engine trouble he should have been transferred to a safer ship in the convoy. Someone was going to suffer for that. Lieutenant Hawkey should have made representations to the Admiral aboard the *Belfast* if the latter hadn't bothered to think about it for himself.

As the following day's dawn once again sent the ship's company to routine action stations, the report came in from the radar cabinet to the bridge.

'Echoes dead ahead, sir. I believe it's the convoy.'

Cameron, once more acting for the Captain, who was

81

confined to his bunk again, acknowledged. He said, 'Keep reporting.'

'Aye, aye, sir.'

Cameron stepped aft to the chart table and ducked his head beneath the canvas screen that shaded the electric light bulb inside. Using parallel rulers and a pair of dividers he established a dead reckoning position from the last star sight and pencilled in a small cross and a neat circle. They were due south of Bear Island now, and into the Barents Sea, with the North Cape rather more than a hundred miles a little east of south. The visibility, though much improved, was not brilliant. There was no wind; the sea lay smooth, almost oily, but there was a heavy swell. The frigate was rolling badly, making life uncomfortable below. Stripey Dander was one of those below, spared from his action station to back up the party watching over the shored-up bulkhead, which was still in reasonably good shape, considering. After the action with the U-boat, more precautions had been taken under the orders of Leyton-Seton – ostensibly; in fact the guiding spirits had been the buffer and the shipwright. Petty Officer Bremner hadn't much of an opinion of that Mr Leyton-Seton, who was stuffed full of airs and graces, shirt cuffs and clean white handkerchiefs. A bit lah-di-dah was Mr Leyton-Seton. He was a fine officer in port, lording it as Officer of the Day and saluting the ladies aboard when the wardroom was entertaining. Some three months earlier the frigate had been in Londonderry for some maintenance work to be carried out, and Leyton-Seton had cleaned for the shore the moment the ship put her nose inside Lough Foyle, when everyone else aboard was still in sweaters, seaboots and duffel-coats. Whilst everyone else had smelled of ten days solid at sea with an Atlantic convoy, Leyton-Seton had smelled like a whore's boudoir. The Captain, then Lieutenant-Commander Stanford, hadn't gone much on that. Bremner had overheard the conversation when Leyton-Seton had arrived on the bridge.

The Captain had lifted his nose in the air and said, 'By God, it's a miracle! We must have arrived early on our ETA.'

'I beg your pardon, sir?' Leyton-Seton had said.

'I smell a chemist's shop. Perhaps its an olfactory mirage since I can't see one.'

'Possibly, sir.'

'On the other hand, perhaps it's you, Leyton-Seton.' The Captain had swung round and raked Leyton-Seton with a stony glare. 'Get off the bridge, man, and hose yourself down.'

Leyton-Seton, looking angry, had gone below. The moment the ship had berthed at Town Quay, just down river from where the Apprentice Boys had locked the gates of the city against catholic James II back in 1689 and thus set the stage for the House of Orange, Leyton-Seton had nipped down the brow and had returned a couple of hours later with a party organized. Petty Officer Bremner, a solid and respectable married man and a good father to two sons, had no objection in the world to young officers letting off steam in between trips to sea, but never in all his born days had he seen the like of what came aboard that evening for the wardroom party. All the floosies in Londonderry by the look of them, painted up to the nines and giggling like all-get-out. The Captain had been invited and for politeness' sake had attended, but he hadn't lasted long. Emerging on to the upper deck, he'd encountered Petty Officer Bremner checking the tightness of the securing wires. They'd exchanged a grin while the Captain mopped at a sweating face. 'God's truth,' Stanford said in amazement. 'I'd never have believed it if I hadn't seen it with my own eyes.'

Bremner laughed. 'Maybe we're just getting older, sir.'

'Saner, I'd call it.' Stanford had gone off to his own cabin and Bremner guessed that, like himself, he was thinking of his wife. Bremner had given a word of thanks to the Almighty that both their wives were still alive; but for how much longer? He knew the skipper had lost a kid.

Bremner came back to the present, the reality of the seamens' messdeck and the bulkhead. Too much water was getting through for his liking, though basically he was sure it was sound enough. He glanced at Able Seaman Dander, taking it easy, taking a rest on a mess table.

He said, 'Get up off your arse, Dander.'

'What for, Buff? I'm –'

'Because I say so. Look at that bloody water! Get rid of it, Dander.'

Grumbling loudly, Dander did so. Squeegee, mop and bloody bucket . . . as usual, he was bloody chokka, pissed-off. Could have been a PO himself by now. If he'd made the effort. If he'd wanted to . . . there were times, now, when he almost wished he had. Life would have been a bit rosier, not so much work. In the Andrew, you stopped work the moment you shipped a hook on your arm as a leading hand. From then on you supervised, which was different. If only he'd realized that years ago. As he mopped up, word reached the damage control party from the bridge: the convoy had been sighted and within the next hour they would be in company.

Bremner said with relief, 'Good-oh!'

Dander didn't comment. Once the convoy was rejoined, the danger of attack would grow.

8

Now the signal lamps were busy. Messages of welcome and enquiry came from the Commodore and from the Senior Officer of the escort in the flagship *Belfast*. Also messages of war's grim toll: the convoy had been attacked by a solitary U-boat, and a merchant ship carrying machine parts had gone to the bottom before the depth charge patterns had been dropped. Hawkey, who had insisted on returning to the bridge when Cameron had passed the word of the radar contact, was glad to be able to report that he had despatched a damaged U-boat, almost certainly the attacker who must have surfaced after the submarine killers had withdrawn towards the convoy. The sinking of the merchant vessel apart, all was sweetness and light, congratulations and the happy proximity of big guns and fast ships.

Then the bombshell was flashed from the *Belfast*: a message received in cypher from the Admiralty had indicated to the Rear-Admiral that the German heavy units reported earlier had moved north between Spitzbergen and Novaya Zemlya in the Barents Sea and with their submarines were believed to be awaiting the oncoming convoy. In their own good time they would move south at speed. The Senior Officer had no current knowledge of the Home Fleet under Admiral Tovey but assumed, hopefully, that the C-in-C would be handy with the *King George V* and his heavy cruisers. In the meantime the only hard fact was that the PQ convoy appeared to be steaming into virtually certain attack by German sea and air forces, the latter likely to come in from the north Norwegian airfields referred to in the Admiralty's earlier signal.

Hawkey looked immensely strained; he was still very tired and Cameron believed he had a temperature. He was shivering violently and could have flu; but he wouldn't go below again, especially now attack loomed. The next signal came from Captain (D) in the destroyer flotilla leader:

Admiral's intentions if engaged are for the convoy to remain together and not repeat not scatter subject only to Commodore's discretion to take avoiding action. Escorts will stand between the convoy and the enemy. Convoy will be joined as soon as possible by reinforcing escorts leaving Archangel.

'Acknowledge,' Hawkey said briefly to the yeoman. 'Add, What about my passengers?' Then he turned to Cameron. 'Why Archangel, I wonder? Why not Murmansk? It's a bloody sight less steaming distance for the reinforcements.'

'No availability there, sir?'

Hawkey nodded. 'I expect that's it, Number One. There never is, is there?' He stared across the flat calm of the sea as the frigate rolled to the swell. Within the next few hours they would make a small alteration to starboard. That made, there would be some three more days to go for Murmansk, *Sprinter*'s own destination. More, for the main body of the convoy to reach Archangel. Days of bitter weather and ferocious attack, days when hope would be all they had to keep them going. The leader was flashing again; shortly after, the yeoman of signals approached with the answer about the passengers, obliquely worded.

'Reply from Senior Officer, sir: Your orders remain for Murmansk and you will break off when given the executive. In the meantime you will continue to act as part of the escort.' The yeoman put his clipboard back beneath his arm. 'Message ends, sir.'

'Thank you, Yeoman.' Hawkey turned to Cameron. 'In other words, bugger the VIP cargo!'

Cameron grinned and said, 'I imagine there was no option, sir. Going off on our own now or during an attack . . . well, if anything's leaked about the passengers, it'd be a dead give-away.'

86

Hawkey glowered. 'Know what I'd like, Number One? I'd like nothing so much as to give away the bloody minister and the bloody marshal. Anyone can have 'em! No charge made.'

They moved ahead. Back in station, Hawkey reduced to convoy speed, and that brought some relief to the hard-pressed collision bulkhead.

To give him his due, no one would have suspected that Fasher was a seething furnace inside; he was no more foul-tempered than normal, no more dangerous to cross. His eye was no more eagle as he went about the ship picking faults and threatening punishment. He knew he had become a detested figure, but he never had been a popular one. Popularity Jacks were, in his view, no good. You didn't get promotion by being popular, you got it by being a bastard and acquiring a reputation for being all seeing and all hearing and never letting anyone get away with anything. He didn't stop to reflect that most admirals were and had been popular officers, that it was perfectly possible to combine efficiency and good officer-like qualities with a decent treatment of the ship's company and a friendly word when it would help. Admirals were a little beyond even Fasher's ambitions. Lieutenant or maybe lieutenant-commander was his ambition – his ceiling, if you like. If Fasher ever thought about Nelson, for instance, it would be as the victor of Trafalgar and the lover of Lady Hamilton, not as the admiral who had prayed for mercy, after victory, in the British Fleet. It had passed Fasher's ken that all the great admirals – Cradock of Coronel, Sturdee, Beatty, Jellicoe, Lord Cork, Sir William Fisher, Sir John Kelly to name a few – had had a good measure of humanity to leaven the snap and autocracy of high command. Fasher was Fasher and found no harm in that, no flaws in his own character. He knew he was a good gunner and had been a good chief gunner's mate. That was enough.

He knew other things but they didn't bother him: he knew the whole ship's company would clam up with sealed lips like Stanley Baldwin if one night in bad weather he was shoved into a metal wash-deck locker, gagged, bound and the locker lid secured with a padlock, and dumped over the side into the fastness of the Barents Sea. In his coffin, lost overboard when lifted by a heavy sea. Rumour said it had happened to other disliked persons in the past, though never, to Fasher's knowledge, to officers. Fasher happened to believe in those rumours; it was so possible, and no one could clam up like a ship's company who thought some of their mates had done the right thing. They could be deaf, blind and dumb and not even the Board of Admiralty could shake them. No evidence, you couldn't prosecute.

Fasher knew also that his wife would have a ball if he didn't come home, if you could call it home. Lil was a washout, dreary and damply tearful most of the time, a drag whose tears would stop only when she boxed him up or heard that he'd bought it at sea. He detested her as much as she detested him, but they'd never thought seriously about divorce. Lil came of a family who wouldn't countenance anything so scandalous as divorce, and as for him, he had his career to think about and there hadn't been the time. Or the money, come to that; chief petty officers rubbed along on around three quid a week all told, plus a miserly marriage allowance. Why had he married her? Simple: he'd been drunk as a fiddler's bitch when he asked her and when he'd sobered up she held something over him: she could get pregnant. She did. Fasher wasn't going to cough up seven-and-six a week on a paternity order and get nothing out of it. Whatever else Lil was, she was a screw. But from that day to this he'd sworn off over-indulgence in liquor, blaming it for sodding up his life. Just a couple, never any more. Fasher had never been drunk again; he had an iron will.

As *Sprinter* took up her position in the escort, Fasher came upon Leading Seaman Holloway making a personal inspection of the paintwork on the after gun-shield. Holloway had a jealous eye for the tiddly appearance of his part-of-ship and at first he wasn't aware of Fasher's approach.

The voice came from behind him, low but tense. 'You've not got away with it, you know.'

Holloway turned and met the mean, close-set eyes. He

said, 'No, I don't suppose I have, because I know you.'

'Sir.' Fasher rose and fell on the balls of his feet, like a copper.

'Sir.'

'That's better. Seeing sense at last, are you, Holloway?'

'Not as far as you're concerned. Sir.'

'You better had. God, you better had!'

'Wouldn't make any difference. You'd still be out to get me. Right?'

Fasher laughed. 'Right. I don't need to tell you this. You've been in the Andrew long enough. I'm an officer now, Holloway. *An officer.* I can make your life bloody hell on earth.'

'And you will.'

'And I will.'

Holloway said, 'Well, that clears the air, as if it needed clearing. Sir. There's just one thing.'

Fasher had been about to turn away. Now he halted and said, 'Well?'

Holloway said with deliberation, as he ran his gloved hand along the gun-shield again, 'Remember Tiny Stack? Petty Officer Stack?'

There was a pause. 'Able Seaman Stack. Yes. So?'

Holloway shrugged. 'Just that he's friend of mine.'

'Go on.' Fasher was staring, his eyes ice-cold, holding a mad look, almost as though he'd guessed what was coming.

'Oh,' Holloway said off-handedly, 'nothing that need concern you. Yet.'

'Meaning?'

Holloway wiped his glove across his nose and met Fasher's stare full on. He said, 'I know something. About the way you faked the charge. Enough to get you court martialled, in retrospect like.' He added, 'If I'd known it at the time, *you*'d have been broken instead of Tiny Stack.'

Breath hissed through Fasher's teeth. 'Do I take it you're threatening me, Leading Seaman Holloway, because if –'

Holloway laughed. 'Nothing was further from my thoughts, *Mr* Fasher. Would I do that to an officer – now *would* I?'

Fasher turned on his heel and stalked away without another word.

Now they were into the real biting cold of the northern winter, the time when nights were long and days were short, the Land of the Midnight Sun in terrible reverse. To come on to the upper deck was torture, and even below the ship was colder than ever.

Cameron found himself spending almost all his time on the bridge even when officially off watch, in order to allow Hawkey to get some sleep. Hawkey was once again badly in need of rest but it was a job to get him to take it. He wasn't taking it now. This was the time when a captain should keep to the bridge, and there was an obstinacy about Hawkey that forced him not to abrogate his responsibilities even though he was disliking his life more and more. He believed himself to be unfitted for command because of the fact that he had to force his mind and body to the task that had dropped upon him. This, Cameron sensed; and knew too that he was being leaned on, used as a prop because – and there was nothing boastful in this – he knew his job. He knew it in a way that neither Leyton-Seton nor Weatherby knew theirs. There was something they lacked and it couldn't be disguised. Fasher knew it, and the senior ratings knew it too. Cameron had been given that extra something, perhaps, because he had been to sea in his father's trawler fleet out of Aberdeen. He'd seen hard times and bad weather, the constant fight of man against the sea, and he'd mixed with men who were amongst the world's finest seamen, hard men all of them. It had rubbed off.

Suddenly Hawkey said, 'Oil fuel, Number One. Just check with the Chief that we've enough to make Murmansk, will you?'

'Aye, aye, sir.' Cameron called the engine-room. If they were getting low, Quince would have said so, and in any case it was a little late by now to refuel from the RFA oilers in company: it wouldn't do to be caught by the German attack, alongside the oiler with the fuel lines connected. Quince answered; sure, they had enough. He sounded surprised at the enquiry, even a little hurt.

Cameron passed his answer to the Captain.

Hawkey ran a hand over his eyes and said, 'Worth checking. When we were stopped . . . fuel was being used to maintain internal services, then we had to make up distance lost. That was an extra, you see.'

'Yes,' Cameron said. It was true enough, certainly.

Hawkey grinned and said, 'Sorry to be a fusspot,' and then his grip on the guardrail slackened and he slid to the deck of the bridge and lay in a crumpled heap.

Cameron was very conscious of the fact that the doctor and the LSBA were dead. He spoke down the voice-pipe to the quartermaster. 'Get the Captain's servant up here, fast. And the boatswain's mate. My compliments to Mr Leyton-Seton. I'd like him to take over the watch for a while.'

Hawkey was staring around vaguely from his bunk and breathing with difficulty. It was a laboured, stertorous sound. His servant had taken his temperature with a thermometer found in the tiny sick bay: it showed 102 degrees. Cameron diagnosed flu with what a doctor might call complications – over-strain and exposure. You didn't normally pass out with simple influenza. For all Cameron knew it might be pneumonia. It was time to be a nuisance to the convoy and ask for assistance; a signal was made to the Senior Officer of the escort, reporting the facts. After some delay the advice of the Surgeon Commander in the *Belfast* was flashed across:

Consider your diagnosis likely. Keep patient in bed on low diet with plenty to drink. Advise aspirins two hourly. Report progress.

Did he mean two aspirins each hour, or one every two hours? Cameron decided it wasn't vital and ordered one every two hours to be on the safe side. Then he went back to the bridge.

'All right?' Leyton-Seton asked.

'I've no idea, really. He doesn't look too good. Parker's

91

looking after him like a mother.' Parker was the Captain's servant, as fussy as an old hen. He would call the bridge in a trice if he got more anxious. Cameron resumed his watch and went into the old routine of convoy work, lifting his binoculars to rake the horizons and try to spot something the lookouts had missed. But there was nothing, just the ships in company, steaming along the route to Russia. The remainder of the day passed peacefully; all they had to fight was the bitter cold. Already the real lasting ice had come and the decks were skating-rinks. Men moving along the upper deck constantly found their feet flying from under them, their only safety the hand-grip on the lifeline. Later that day Stripey Dander was one of the victims. Going on watch for the first dog his seaboots skidded away and at the same moment his gloved hand came off the lifeline. Yelling blue murder, he slid on his bottom towards the starboard guardrail, which didn't happen to be there since the ship had been stripped for action already. He saw the jaws of death looming, a very cold death in the icy Barents Sea. Then he was jerked suddenly to a stop. He lay gasping in fright and saw a pair of leather seaboots beside him. As his gaze travelled upwards he saw Mr Fasher.

Fasher's face was as hard as the ice and as cold. He said, 'Get up off your backside, Dander. Call yourself a seaman, you're a bloody useless lump of fat-arsed currant bun.'

'Yessir!' Dander got shakily to his feet, found his arm taken and the hand guided to the lifeline.

'Grab it. Don't let go of it. And get some of that fat off.' Fasher, like a side of beef himself, strode away, grasping the lifeline. Rotten bastard, Dander thought resentfully, but he'd saved his life. Maybe he wasn't so bad after all. He'd taken a risk on his own life; Dander knew himself to be quite a weight.

As Dander proceeded shakily on towards his place of duty, things were happening elsewhere. The Captain's condition was now giving cause for real concern: the temperature was up, and stood at 104 despite the aspirins and such liquid as could be got down his throat. The light was starting to fade in the sky and a bitter east wind from across the top of Siberia was beginning to whip up the sea so that slivers of ice, rather than simple spray, cut viciously into the men on watch. To lift one's face against it, to maintain that vital lookout, was torture. The wind looked like worsening. After words with Parker and a sight of Hawkey moving restlessly in his bunk, face dead white with violent red patches, Cameron knew he had to ask for more than just signalled advice, and he had to do it before the night came down and the weather deteriorated further. A signal was made to the Senior Officer asking for a medical officer to be sent across. The response was immediate: Close my starboard side at once.

Cameron said, 'Port ten.' Weatherby, on watch now, passed the order. 'Send down to the buffer, Weatherby. Hands to stand by port to take the doctor from the Flag.'

Weatherby said, 'Aye, aye, sir.' The 'sir' was an automatic response to authority; there was nothing sardonic in it. Efficiently, as though to the manner born, Cameron conned the frigate towards the great side of the cruiser, reducing speed as he came up to nose his shattered bows in for where he saw the jumping-ladder being put over the side. Nearer and nearer . . . sea spouted up between the two ships, showered the decks and instantly froze. A duffel-coated figure stood at the head of the ladder, clutching a bag. This was a devil of a way for the doctor to call, Cameron thought with a grin. He wouldn't be relishing his trip down that swaying ladder . . . a far cry from a nice, warm car with a couple of guineas waiting together with a glass of something to keep the cold out! Cameron became aware of another duffel-coated figure with a brass hat, a double row of brass, leaning from the bridge wing. The Admiral brought up a megaphone and shouted down to the quarterdeck.

'Fast as you can, down there.' He shifted target. '*Sprinter* ahoy!'

'Yes, sir?'

'Dr Matthews will have to stay with you till you reach Murmansk. My radar reports contact with ships ahead. I suspect the enemy. Get away from my side soonest possible. And good luck to you.'

Cameron called back, 'My passengers, sir. Should I transfer them?'

'No,' the answer came, forcefully. 'You'll keep to your orders. It's my hope the Hun'll leave you alone – you don't look worth another shell, frankly!' The Admiral paused. 'You – what's your name and rank?'

'Cameron, sir, Lieutenant RNVR.'

'I'll remember it. I like your ship-handling.'

The Admiral withdrew. The doctor came down the ladder, making heavy weather of it. The moment he had got his feet on the deck he was grabbed by a party of seamen under the chief boatswain's mate and Cameron passed the orders for taking the frigate clear, and back into her convoy station. As he dropped astern, the warning signals were already being flashed to the ships in company.

9

THE information was terse: what must clearly be the German heavy units were twenty-five miles to the north-east and closing at high speed. The convoy was meeting them at a combined speed of something like forty-five knots and battle would be joined within the next thirty minutes. It was expected that a U-boat pack would join in; also that the aerial attack from the German-held airfields in northern Norway, lying less now than a hundred miles to the south of the convoy's position, would be a strong one.

By this time wireless silence had been broken from the *Belfast*. The enemy knew they were there so there was nothing to be gained by not alerting the Admiralty. The Rear-Admiral had passed a full report and although nothing specific was said in the acknowledgement, in the hopes that the position of Admiral Tovey's ships was not known to the German command, the Rear-Admiral knew what orders would go at once in cypher to Tovey. There was no reason why he should not hearten the men of the convoy and its escort and as the warships increased speed to obey the previous order and put themselves between the convoy and the enemy, he proceeded to do so.

'Signal, sir,' Cameron's yeoman reported. A light was flashing from the *Belfast*'s signal bridge. Soon the yeoman reported again. 'From the Flag, sir: Keep your peckers up. Admiral Tovey will be steaming for us with the Home Fleet, sir.'

Cameron nodded. Admiral Sir John Tovey's ships would include the aircraft-carrier *Victorious*, ready to fly off her

95

squadrons of rather sad old Swordfish torpedo-bombers, the well-tried biplanes known throughout the fleet as Stringbags. Old they might be, but they were still capable of good service; in one of them not so long ago Lieutenant-Commander Esmonde had won a posthumous VC for stopping the great *Bismarck* in her tracks, or at any rate slowing her so that she could be caught by the battleships and cruisers. In a sense, the Stringbags had avenged the mighty battle-cruiser *Hood*.

Throughout the ship, now at action stations, men waited for the big moment, all of them knowing that they could be facing their personal end. The escorts were small enough; even the *Belfast* with her turreted six-inch guns – twelve of them in all – and her heavy anti-aircraft armament and her six 21-inch torpedo tubes – to say nothing of three aircraft launched by catapult – would be hard put to it to engage the heavy ships successfully. Those ships were believed to be the fifteen-inch gunned battleship *Hohenzollern* with the heavy cruisers *Köln* and *Mühldorf*; and they would have a destroyer screen with them. No easy battle; if Tovey didn't close in time the Nazis would go through the convoy like a knife through butter. Cameron thought of the merchant-ship crews who were relying on the escort: they were the bravest ones, those who steamed on, manning bridges and engine-rooms, who steamed phlegmatically through blood and shell with their vital cargoes, kept on going come hell or high water – utterly unable to hit back except with a few popguns manned by naval ratings or soldiers of the Royal Artillery. Civilians still, they deserved every man's respect.

The minutes ticked away.

Weatherby said suddenly, 'No more orders. From the Senior Officer, I mean.'

Cameron glanced at him. The voice had sounded shaky. He said, shrugging, 'No need. Passed already. We stick together and we fight through.'

'We bloody well sink, you mean.'

'Oh, we'll survive, old man.'

'Like hell. Think of those guns.'

'Better not to,' Cameron said. 'Sometimes, imagination's

useful. At others it's best kept down. Hope's the thing. That, and sticking to it.'

'For what? The Russians?'

'No.' Cameron turned and faced Weatherby squarely through the gathering night, the night that would soon be lit like an inferno by the gun-flashes and the exploding merchant ships with their lethal cargoes of oil fuel and high explosive. 'Not just for the Russians . . . not really. For ourselves. We're all part of one war, after all. If the Russians go down, so probably do we. They're engaging Hitler. That's good. We don't want Hitler landing on the south coast.' He paused. 'Your home's in Worthing, isn't it?'

Weatherby nodded. 'Yes.'

'Well, then, just think about it. Keep on thinking about it when those guns open. And don't think about anything else – except the ship, and my orders. All right?'

'Yes, sir,' Weatherby said.

Below along the upper deck, and below again wherever the ship's company was dispersed at their various stations, Fasher also was doing some stiffening. In a ship now officered in effect solely by the RNVR except for himself and Quince, who was a mere engineer, he felt stiffening was needed. You never knew, he told himself, which way a basic civilian would jump when the crunch came, and the crunch was on its way all right. Big ships were big ships and enough said. Fasher hadn't spent his whole career on the parade ground at Pompey, or at Whale Island – a lot of it, but not all. As a Seaman Boy Second Class he'd been at Jutland under Jellicoe and had come under the fire from the battle-cruisers of the German High Seas Fleet. Then aged fourteen and a bit, he'd been dead scared. They were all scared as the big shells hit or screamed overhead; that was natural. Fasher had almost forgotten – because he didn't want to think about it – that although they'd all been scared he had been the only one to his knowledge to do some skrimshanking. When his cruiser had been hit and a number of casualties caused in his vicinity he had found an opportunity to vamoose, to be absent, as the service put it, from his place of duty. It had been daft, of course, because you were never safe anywhere in a ship in action, but he hadn't been experienced enough to realize it then; anyway, he'd hidden himself away in the lee of a shattered bulkhead once the damage control parties had moved on and he'd nursed an arm torn by a shell splinter, not badly but bloodily. When action was brought to an end by the bugler of the Royal Marine Light Infantry sounding the cease-fire, Seaman Boy II Fasher had emerged into the light of day streaming his blood and collapsing in a convincing faint. After that, he'd been treated as a minor hero. The Boy Stood On The Burning Deck . . . almost. He'd enjoyed that. The sneaking sense of shame stayed with him for a while, but not for very long. Of course, since then he'd changed. Daft to say he enjoyed action, but he knew he could stand up to it. He'd proved that, even aboard this dead-end frigate. And back in World War I he'd seen more action after Jutland and had stood up to that as well. Fourteen and a bit that first time . . . what could you expect?

But the fact that he'd once been shit scared had the odd effect of making him harder than ever on those who might also be shit scared when the time came. So he dealt with them in advance, concentrating on the younger ones, the hostilities-only ordinary seamen, the erstwhile civilians who couldn't possibly have any guts if they tried.

'You lot,' he said to three of them manning Number One gun under Leading Seaman Trott. 'What's coming is what you joined for. There's nothing to it if you're men. You'll be all right unless your number's on the projectile when it hits. If you're scared enough to run, then the proj'll follow you and catch you up, right?' He paused. 'Well, one of you answer.'

'Yes, sir,' one of them said.

'Good! And if it doesn't catch you up, then you know who will: me. If any man among my guns' crews swings the lead or shows a yellow streak, then I'll have him. I'll have him for cowardice in face of the enemy, I'll have him for *desertion* in face of the enemy. That's a promise. You, there.' He dug a gloved hand into the chest of the OD who'd just answered him. 'Know what the laid down punishment is for that, do

98

you?'

'I – I'm not sure, sir –'

'I am,' Fasher said. He paused, then made a grim joke. 'One day's death,' he said, and moved on towards his next target. The OD asked Leading Seaman Trott if what Mr Fasher had said was true and Trott said it was, up to a point. 'Shall suffer death' was still in the Articles of War but no one had received death this century to his knowledge.

'Don't you worry your nut about that bloody barrack stanchion, lad,' Trott said loudly. He might be dead himself within the next twenty minutes and then he'd be beyond Fasher's nasty talons. He might as well let Fasher know what he thought of him before he went. But by this time Fasher was at it again with another pep-talk and listening closely to the sound of his own voice.

Below in the engine-room and in the boiler-rooms there was too much noise for easy speech and the artificers and stokers watched their dials and gauges mostly in silence. Handfuls of cotton-waste were used automatically to wipe down wherever dirt or a spot of grease showed; engine-rooms were usually one of the cleanest parts of a ship and the black gang knew that Mr Quince wouldn't want to go into action with his machinery looking like a scran-bag. Quince was on the starting-platform in a clean pair of white overalls and even a clean white cap cover over his officer's cap in place of the filthy article that engineers normally wore below. Quince was thinking again of his wife and wondering if she would soon be free of him. His mind went back into the past, to that bar in Devonport. In Fore Street it had been, and he'd been serving in the old *Cumberland*, sister ship of the *Durham* in company with them now. Nessie had been lovely, great big knockers and fair hair, shingled. He'd liked the movement of her bottom when she walked, a sort of waggle that did all kinds of things to a young ERA 3. Well, Quince thought with a sigh, marry in haste and repent at leisure. He hadn't waited; she had no parents to ask and she didn't mind shifting to Pompey. They married in Devonport, then he took her home. Quince's parents had been stunned when they set eyes on her;

99

though they hadn't said anything, the shock and horror could be sensed and Quince, reacting as any young man would, had seen little of them since then. When they'd died within weeks of each other, he'd been racked with remorse, because by that time he knew they'd been right in their unspoken assessment. Pride had kept him away: he wasn't going to admit that Nessie had waggled her bottom for all and sundry.

On the starting-platform the sound-powered telephone from the bridge whined at him. He answered. 'Chief here.'

'Cameron. Just to keep you informed, Chief. *Belfast* and *Durham* have moved ahead of the convoy, with the destroyers. We're staying with the corvettes to act as anti-submarine guard.'

Quince said, 'Right you are, Mr Cameron. And thanks.'

The line went dead. Quince rubbed his chin thoughtfully and passed the message to the Chief ERA for onward transmission to the lads. That Cameron: hadn't even quite got used to calling himself the First Lieutenant and now he was as good as in command. Modest, was young Cameron. And reliable, Quince felt. He didn't like going into action under RNVR command, but if that had to be, then Cameron was a good choice. You didn't get a DSC for sod-all. It was a funny world: not much more than eighteen months ago, Cameron had been an OD in a destroyer and in one bound as it were he'd zoomed over the heads of men like himself with bloody years and years of service in. Quince grinned at a related thought: he'd zoomed over Fasher's head and all. Quince rather liked that, knowing full well, because Fasher had said as much, that it made the gunner's blood boil every time he so much as looked at Cameron.

Above the engine-room, in the small cabin that was now his sole refuge since the wardroom had been shattered, Marshal Yurigin stared at the heavy steel deadlight clamped over the glass of the port. Somewhere beyond lay the great land mass of the USSR with its armies fighting for their lives and for the deliverance of Stalingrad and Moscow from the Nazi threat. If this convoy should be lost, the blow would be grievous and it would be as well if he, Yurigin, were lost with it. Its loss

100

would scarcely be his fault but Comrade Generalissimo Stalin was a hard man who, like Hitler himself, liked to have a scapegoat. Yurigin would not be executed, nor sent to Siberia and the salt mines, but he would be disgraced, his name forever associated with failure. Yes, Comrade Stalin was a hard man and often – be it admitted ever so secretly – a boorish and vindictive one.

The convoy must not be lost but it was virtually certain that at any rate most of it would be. Unless the British Admiral Tovey arrived in time with his battle fleet. . .

There was a knock at the cabin door.

'Who is it?' Yurigin asked.

'Prynn.'

'Then enter.'

Harcourt Prynn came in. He was looking a very sick man, Yurigin thought, as scared as a child on seeing a bull. Unbidden, the Englishman sat down and tried to hide the shake in his hands, his thighs, his everything. The man was a coward, Yurigin thought. His upbringing had been soft, like cottonwool. Yurigin's had not. His father had worked in an iron foundry in Leningrad, then called St Petersburg. The old man had been one of the early Bolsheviks. Yurigin himself had been a trooper of the Czar until he had joined in the Bloody Sunday storming of the Winter Palace. It had not been easy on the body or the spirit to be a trooper of the hated Czar. Yurigin had endured many punishments as was the lot of any soldier, loyal or otherwise, and his back still carried the scars of the lash, which was a different thing from the application of a light cane to Harcourt Prynn's bottom by a schoolmaster. Harcourt Prynn now wanted the solace of company when all the ship's personnel were otherwise engaged. When action started he would help out with the injured as ordered by the Captain. So would Yurigin. But for now he was lonely and Yurigin felt a desire to tease.

Sombrely he said, placing big hands on his knees and staring hard at the British minister, 'From life to death is a quick transition. Do not worry. You will know little.'

'I don't want to die. It seems such a waste.'

101

'Of your knowledge and position?'

'Well.' Harcourt Prynn fiddled with his tie; he was as well-dressed as if he'd been about to attend a meeting of the cabinet. Yurigin was wearing a smock like a peasant. 'There's so much to be done, isn't there?'

'Yes,' Yurigin said, 'that is true.' Suddenly the desire to tease left him. Harcourt Prynn might be British and a capitalist but currently they were both facing the same danger. 'So much yet to do, so many advances to be made. I believe we shall come through. If there is a God, which may be the case though I personally do not think so, then he will have mercy on the Russian people and bring them through to the light of the day when the war is won. Since the war will not be won without guns and tanks and explosives and oil fuel, I believe he will help us to reach Russia. There, my friend, is not that a good and happy thought?'

Harcourt Prynn didn't respond; he went on shaking. Yurigin felt angry. The British were rotten through and through and the moment the war was won they would turn against the USSR. They must not be allowed to do so.

The night was as dark as pitch, no glimmer of moon or stars. The wind was increasing as Cameron had expected, buffeting the small ships of the escort as they pitched and rolled. The ice was lethal. *Sprinter*, in the rear of the convoy, had already lost a man overboard, a man who had slid on a heavy roll from the fore gun-mounting and had gone before anyone could give him a hand. Cameron had taken a calculated risk and turned the ship to make a search, but he might just as well not have stuck his neck out. The man would have died within minutes and in any case he couldn't be seen. There was just an empty lifebuoy cast by Leading Seaman Trott. It was likely the man's own inflatable lifebelt hadn't been blown up. They were uncomfortable to wear and some people took chances.

Ten minutes later a signal came by light from the Rear-Admiral. Cameron's yeoman reported, 'From the Flag, sir, have enemy in sight.'

Cameron nodded. The Captain would want to know but

102

Cameron hoped he wouldn't come to the bridge. If he did, it would be the end of him. He called the wheelhouse and sent a messenger to Hawkey. Then the gunfire started ahead. The flashes could be seen, the heavy rumble heard as the strong wind bore it along to the convoy. The wind was strengthening fast; Cameron was glad enough of that. It would put paid to the U-boat pack, or at least make their task much harder. As in the Atlantic, so here in the far northern waters the U-boats tended to stay deep below the bad weather, though tonight they might well take risks in the interest of the grand strategy to destroy a vital convoy. Meanwhile the merchant ships plodded on, invisible except as darker blurs in the night, rolling and pitching to the waves and the swell, shepherded and guarded by the wind-tossed corvettes. Cameron's mind was upon his passengers: they, he knew, were to be his first concern rather than the convoy itself. As matters developed there would be fast decisions to be made.

Ahead, there was a big explosion, a brilliant sheet of red and orange flame. Cameron had his binoculars up and was focussed, by chance, on the exact spot. He could see the whirl of debris, black and sinister in the flames outlining a three-island cargo vessel. Metal and bodies would be in that lot. A sacrifice for Russia. And soon after that the heavy throb of the German bombers was heard, coming in from the south.

Under very heavy fire the Rear-Admiral took the *Belfast* ahead to come down on the German flagship, the battleship *Hohenzollern*. He had closed dangerously to within torpedo range and amidships the lieutenant(T) was waiting for the order to fire. Beside him was the torpedo gunner. The latter was not there for much longer. Raking fire came from the *Hohenzollern*, returning the salvo from the cruiser's six-inch turrets. A shell from the German's secondary armament took the midship casing between the funnels and a metal splinter entered the torpedo gunner's back and came out through his chest. Seconds later the chief torpedo gunner's mate also bought it. Then the order came from the Admiral's bridge

103

and the lieutenant(T) lifted his voice in a shout.

'*Fire one . . . fire two . . . fire three!*'

Amid clouds of smoke from the propellant charges the tin fish shot from the tubes and plopped down into the sea. As the torpedoes left the cruiser, the German had been brought on the port bow and was still some half-mile ahead and closing. In theory the cigar-shaped killers should strike as they headed to cross her course. But in such weather conditions as existed it was a gamble that was weighted against them. A sound of disgust went up from the torpedomen as all the fish were seen to miss: the *Hohenzollern* steamed on, her guns firing without cease. Along the *Belfast*'s decks the damage appeared to be collosal: boats had vanished from the davits in a shower of smashed woodwork; the mainmast was down in a tangle of wire rigging and smashed aerials. The after six-inch turret had taken a direct hit from the *Hohenzollern*'s main armament and had vanished to leave a gaping hole in the upper deck as a result of the explosion having reached the shell handling room below. Fire raged upwards through torn metal and blazing woodwork, and there was a stench of burning flesh. It was like the red fires of hell, an open crematorium. Dead and wounded lay along the decks as the fire parties did what they could to fight the flames; sick-berth attendants, under the doctors, worked wonders as they gave pain-killing injections in face of the lash and fury of the German gunners. And the *Belfast* fought on; her remaining turrets engaged the enemy to good effect.

Away to starboard, one of the destroyer escort blew sky-high, shattered and broken in half by a salvo from the heavy guns of the *Mühldorf*. Soon after this, as the first wave of bombers roared in, another explosion came: this time it was the *Köln*. The German cruiser had been steaming to starboard of her own flagship, and she had crossed the track of the *Belfast*'s torpedoes. No one could say how many had hit, but the *Köln* was seen in the binoculars on the *Belfast*'s bridge to be listing heavily to port and to be on fire. That fire spread with amazing rapidity: flames shot high and the watchers from the British ships saw the proud German naval battle ensigns, the stark and gory emblems of Nazidom, take fire and curl away into cinders scattered by the wind. The *Köln* began turning in circles as though her steering had gone; in all probability one of the tin fish had taken her stern. She slowed, still circling.

The Rear-Admiral passed his orders to his flag captain in a steady voice. 'Shift target. We'll finish off the *Köln* by gunfire and then concentrate on the *Mühldorf*. Chief Yeoman, make to the *Durham*, intercept *Hohenzollern* immediately.'

By now the sea was dappled with waterspouts as the German bombers released their loads. They were concentrating, Cameron saw, on the merchant ships, leaving the opposed surface forces to fight it out on their own. The night became day as an ammunition carrier was hit on her bridge, and then took another bomb slap on the hatches of her Number Two hold for'ard. The concussion was tremendous, sweeping hot swathes of air across the water. It could be felt like a savage blow on *Sprinter*'s bridge. Men reeled from its force. One explosion succeeded another, and the vast flames showed the ship glowing red-hot and settling in two halves, bow and stern pointing upward, the two inward ends digging into the foaming water; then she was gone in a great uprush of steam and displaced sea. No man would have lived through that. Sick at heart, Cameron swung his glasses away from the agony. He saw two more ships go in lesser explosions and then he was twisting and turning the frigate as enemy aircraft passed overhead, their big bomb doors swinging open.

10

HAWKEY had not come to the bridge. The Surgeon Lieutenant from the flagship had doped him down and that was that. He didn't stir while the bombs and guns lit the night's darkness with savagery, whilst men went to terrible and agonizing death in water overlaid with the thick treacle of oil fuel spilled from bunkers or with flame that spread from a tanker that had blown up and spilled blazing aviation spirit. Cameron had watched in helpless horror as the big tanker had turned into a firework, with brilliant spurts of flame shooting out in all directions from a central ball of fire that gave the grotesque appearance of a burning Strewelpeter whose head of spiky hair had leapt from a wicked fairy tale to bedevil men in the Barents Sea. In that terrible ball of flame the crew would have fried instantly.

By now the ships of the convoy had scattered, the Commodore exercising the option left him by the Rear-Admiral. The target had to be dispersed, at least within the overall framework of the escort. Cameron's Oerlikon guns were in action, stuttering their racketty defiance at the JU 88s, pumping their 20mm shells towards the great sinister underbellies, keeping the aircraft high as they were picked up and held by the searchlights. Two came down close by *Sprinter*'s starboard side, hit by the heavy ack-ack from the cruisers. One blew up on impact, and the frigate's decks were swept by a hail of splinters. By some miracle no one was killed; but something heavy took Weatherby in the back and he skidded and fell. His forehead hit the binnacle and the result was concussion. He was removed below by a stretcher party. Elsewhere in the ship the flying jags caused a number of cuts. Leading Seaman Holloway was one who suffered: a piece of metal sliced right through the back of his duffel coat, low down – sliced right through his trousers and cut right across his buttocks. He didn't notice it at the time, but he did when a lull came and he knew he wouldn't sit down for a week or more. Already his long johns, the thick grey woollen underpants issued to all men serving in northern waters in winter, were wet with blood. It was a small thing and Holloway gave thanks for the luck that had kept his rear pointing the way it had. He'd heard of a chief yeoman of signals who hadn't been so lucky and had suffered a non-fatal but very serious loss. Fleetingly, he wondered if it was grounds for divorce; he was wondering this when he became aware of something astern and he looked up and saw one of the Nazi bombers, very low and with flames streaking from its engines. Holloway gasped and ran for cover, if there was any cover. The bomber looked as though it was about to pancake on the *Sprinter*.

It did. Almost, anyway. It took the quarterdeck right aft. One engine finished up against the bulkhead of the after screen, hard up against the wreckage of the wardroom. There was a burst of flame. The port wing broke off, the starboard one cracked but remained more or less attached. The front part of the aircraft sat firmly along the quarterdeck, the rear end and the tail sagged down into the water immediately over the rudder and propellors. Somewhere under the body were the depth charges in their racks.

Holloway picked himself up from the deck and ran aft, dangerously, slithering on the ice. Someone passed him, going for'ard and looking as white as a ghost: Fasher. Holloway grinned sardonically and continued aft.

Fasher went up the bridge ladder like greased lightning. As he got there, the fire parties were already going aft at Cameron's order. Fasher screamed out a warning about the depth charges. There was fire down aft, he yelled, bloody fire.

'All right, Guns,' Cameron said. He sounded steady but he

felt the shake in his hands. It was touch and go now.

'It's not all right at all,' Fasher said harshly. 'If the TNT goes up we've bloody had it! And there could be bombs aboard that aircraft too –'

'They'd have gone up on impact, Guns.'

'I wouldn't bank on it, Mr Cameron. The only hope's that she'd dropped her load. You'll have to do something fast now.'

'You're the expert, Guns. What's your advice?'

'My advice?' Fasher stared, his face working. 'My advice is to abandon and bloody fast at that. You can get the seaboat away, and the motor-boat and the rafts. If you hurry.'

Cameron said, 'I'm not abandoning. That's suicide and you know it.'

'I don't know any such thing. It's bloody suicide to stay aboard. Someone'd pick us up from the boats.'

Cameron looked aft. The hoses were in action now, pumping water into the blazing aircraft engine. Someone, the buffer Cameron believed, was wielding an axe. The sea was wild now, the wind had grown heavier. The tops of the waves were being taken and blown in spindrift that lay like a sheet across the disturbed water. Even in a boat no one would live for long, and those allocated to the Carley floats might just as well start digging their own graves.

Cameron said, 'I'm not abandoning, Guns.'

'You asked my advice. I gave it.' Fasher's voice was a shout still. 'I don't reckon you've the experience for command, Cameron. Where's the Captain?'

'Very sick. Not to be disturbed –'

'He'll be disturbed in a moment, all right! When that lot blows he'll go up with it, so will all of us. I'm going to pass the order to abandon.' Fasher made across the bridge for the tannoy, eyes wild in the red light still coming from the burning remains of the tanker.

Cameron gestured to Leyton-Seton, who had taken over from Weatherby as action Officer of the Watch. Leyton-Seton understood well enough and acted quickly. He wrapped his arms around the gunner and held him fast.

Leyton-Seton was stronger than he looked, and he had been taught a thing or two at Eton where a fellow had had to look after himself on occasions.

'Steady, old boy,' he said amiably. 'You were about to disobey the Captain's orders. It doesn't do, you know. I won't let you go till you promise to behave.' He winked at Cameron.

'Christ, you bugger, you're still wet behind the ears,' Fasher said through his teeth, not shouting now. He'd been shaken to the core at having hands laid upon him. Why, it was a court martial offence.

Leyton-Seton grinned and said, 'Well, now, I think it's you who is wet behind the ears, Mr Fasher. Respectable gunners don't behave like this. They've grown out of it. You ought to be ashamed of yourself. Something tells me you're only an acting gunner. You're going to need a recommend to get your confirmation . . . aren't you?'

Fasher kept still. The voice of sanity spoke to him and penetrated. He'd made an exhibition of himself, and in the hearing of ratings too – a lot of it would have gone straight down the voice-pipe to the Chief QM on the wheel, and his wheelhouse staff. He said viciously, 'Know it all, don't you!'

'More than you think,' Leyton-Seton said in a quiet voice, and released his captive.

Cameron said, 'Let's forget it, Guns. Go down aft and take charge, there's a good chap.'

'Good chap, eh. Some people!'

'It was an order, Guns. Just see to it.'

Fasher turned on his heel and left the bridge. The racket all around the frigate was appalling; another ship went up in a roar of smoke and flame as he reached the foot of the ladder. Way ahead there was another explosion right on the heels of the last, and Fasher saw three slim funnels outlined in the glare, two masts, four eight-inch gun-turrets . . . the stern was lifting clear of the water, so was the bow. It was the *Durham*, and her back was broken. In his imagination Fasher could hear the screams of dying men, the useless thrash of limbs as the battened-down occupants in the steel shafts leading from the gun-turrets to the shell-handling rooms filled with water either from the order to flood or from fractured plates. Already World War I had come back to Mr Fasher, that fear that had gripped him as a Seaman Boy Second Class was back with him. It was Seaman Boy II Fasher that turned aside before the gunner reached the quarterdeck.

'Right *there*, Buff – see?' Holloway pointed the way for the axe. He was drenched with sweat as well as with the blood congealing in his long johns and there was a smell of burning wool from his duffel coat. The blaze in the aircraft engine was obstinate and was still getting the better of the fire hoses. Not only that but it was spreading aft along the wrecked fuselage. In the cockpit, half hanging over the port side, two dead Germans slowly burned and added a pungent stench as the flesh melted and ran down. Another Jerry had climbed from the hanging tail, emerging from the sea like Father Neptune trailing blood instead of seaweed. He hadn't been noticed in the general confusion until he'd climbed over the port wing of his aircraft and, reaching the top of the midship superstructure by the searchlight platform, had met Able Seaman Dander.

Stripey had stared. 'Where the buggery 'ave *you* come from?' he asked.

The Jerry, not badly hurt, was supercilious. He spoke good English. 'That is a so stupid question, very English.'

'So's this,' Stripey said, and fetched him off one, smack in the kisser. The bugger had done his best to kill him, Stripey knew. The Jerry went down flat, looking astonished. Stripey muttered to himself, bent and helped him to his feet. They were all doing their duty. But this was a Hun, so Stripey gave him a piece of his mind. 'Bloody 'Itler. Stupid carpet-chewing bastard . . . and don't bleedin' well answer me back, I'm *British* and we're going to 'ave you sods licked before much bloody longer.'

'I think you are a fool if you believe that. The Führer –'

'Ah, stuff it,' Stripey said in disgust. He was about to add something further when the tannoy came alive, loudly.

110

Cameron's voice, the acting skipper and good luck to him . . . and all Stripey Dander's rather incoherent patriotism rose to the back of his throat, chokingly, when Cameron said: 'Admiral Tovey with the Home Fleet is joining from the west. That is all.'

The tannoy had scarcely clicked off again when Tovey proved that he was there all right. The immense boom of the fourteen-inch guns beat through against the wind and within minutes Tovey's flagship *King George V* became visible in the gun-flashes as the salvoes were hurled across the convoy to find their targets in the German line.

'See?' Stripey said. '*Now* you're going to watch a lovely fuckin' battle!'

Holloway and Petty Officer Bremner had also heard the tannoy but were too busy to get excited about it. Tovey or not, the old *Sprinter* was still in appalling danger. The buffer had smashed away with his axe where Holloway had indicated and some progress had been made. Some of the wrecked underbelly had been hacked clear as the result of prodigious effort while the fire parties concentrated on dousing the flames before they could creep back to the depth charges. There was a hell of a lot of explosive around and if it went up the stern would be blown off and a lot more ship with it, not that Holloway or Bremner would know much about that. It would be a quick way to go, a quick way out from under Fasher's dirty tricks department. Holloway, burrowing through towards the charges, flung a word over his shoulder.

'Seen Mr Fasher, Buff?'

'Not a bloody sign.' Bremner went on swinging with his axe. No orders had reached them from the bridge; Fasher might have brought them, but Fasher hadn't come aft – no matter, what they were doing was what the skipper would have ordered: get at the bloody charges and get them overboard, fast as possible.

Bremner hacked away. The axe-work was tiring for a man who was no longer young, but he hardly noticed that. He believed he was gaining on the fire and he better bloody had

. . . when it got further aft, he'd be forced to break off, he wouldn't be able to work with it right above his head and burning down towards him, though he would try as long as possible to give Holloway his chance to grab the lever and drop the charges – or manhandle them out of the racks and throwers if he couldn't operate the lever. Bremner could only make a wild guess at how long it might be before sheer heat did something nasty to the TNT. It wasn't particularly unstable, he knew that much, but there had to come a time when it would succumb.

'How's it going, Holloway?'

'Getting there,' Holloway said.

Victorious was with the Home Fleet and had flown off her aircraft. The Stringbags came lumbering in, making a wide sweep away from the convoy to turn and attack the German heavy ships. *Hohenzollern* had suffered damage from the batteries aboard the *Belfast* and *Durham* before the latter had gone, but was in full fighting trim, as was the *Mühldorf* and most of the destroyers. Fulmar fighters from *Victorious* were also in the air and weaving around the JU 88s. The tide had turned in the British favour now; the *King George V* was a formidable proposition and Tovey's cruisers had the legs of the Germans. But it was still a long running fight and the dawn came wet and blustering in the eastern sky before the *Hohenzollern*, slowed like the *Bismarck* by a torpedo attack from the Stringbags, was caught by a salvo from the British flagship and blew up with an explosion that seemed to split the very skies.

'Magazines,' Cameron said. He steadied his glasses on two of the attacking Stringbags returning to the carrier, to be rearmed probably. Gallant old planes, all struts and canvas – any amount of rigging, like an old sailing ship, stalling speed ninety knots, slow as carthorses – but they'd made rings round the Jerries. Cameron waved in salute as the Stringbags went past his beam. A gloved hand waved back from each, giving the thumbs-up sign. There were grins beneath the goggles; they were that close. The pilots couldn't hear him

112

but Cameron called out, 'Bloody well done!'

That was about it. The remaining German ships turned their tails and went off at speed, heading north, deeper into the iron-hard arctic circle. Tovey sent his cruisers in chase, but with orders not to press it further than twenty miles; they were needed in defence of the convoy, for another attack could come from the air. Meanwhile the JU 88s had also broken off, turning back for north Norway to report only partial success. Now the signal lamps were busy, exchanging information, adding up the cost. It had been heavy: as well as the *Durham* three destroyers had been sunk, and four of the corvettes. One corvette had been disabled and the Rear-Admiral was ordering a destroyer to pass a tow. As for the convoy, it was tragedy for hundreds of merchant seamen and for the Russian war effort: no less than twenty-two heavily laden ships had gone, leaving only pathetic wreckage and corpses, now sunk but to rise again later, to mark their passing.

Cameron said, 'Get a report from aft, Leyton-Seton.'

'I've been trying. There's still no answer from the phone.'

'Send a messenger . . . no, wait. I'll go myself. Take over, will you.' Cameron left the bridge and made his way aft. From what he could see, the fire was out. That spelled safety. Half-way along the deck he met Petty Officer Bremner, coming for'ard and looking green.

'Well, Buffer?'

Bremner gave a weary salute; he was moving like a zombie and his sea clothing, scarcely identifiable as uniform, was in tatters and filthy tatters at that. There was a lot of blood. He said, 'We got some of the charges over, sir, while the aircraft was still burning. That is, Holloway did . . . deserves the bloody VC if you ask me, sir. When the fire was out, we stopped like. Didn't seem no more point.'

Cameron nodded. 'Right. All's well that ends well. Now we just have to clear away the debris.'

'Yes, sir.' Bremner wiped the back of a hand across his eyes. The hand, Cameron noticed, was shaking. Too much axe work. Bremner went on in a dead-sounding voice. 'And

113

Holloway, sir. What's left.'

Cameron's eyes widened, looking a question. Bremner said, 'There was a roll and the bloody plane shifted. Holloway was underneath, trying to move across to the starboard racks. The lot collapsed on him, the bloody lot . . . he was skewered.'

Cameron went on aft.

Holloway's legs were visible, motionless, at an awkward angle. He lay like a moth that had been removed from a killing bottle and mounted on a pin.

Surgeon Lieutenant Matthews came to the bridge, looking seasick. A frigate's motion was very different from that of a cruiser and the seas were high still. *Sprinter* was rolling like a cow. The wind was sharp as a whiplash and the doctor was muffled to the eyebrows so that he looked like a moving ball of wool. He said, 'Your Captain's pulling through –'

'Thank God for that,' Cameron said.

'Not fit for duty, though.'

'Have you told him that, Doctor?'

Matthews grinned and said, 'Yes, I have. He doesn't like it.'

'Like a bet? For my money he'll be up here any minute.'

Matthews shook his head. 'He won't, you know –'

'You don't know Hawkey!'

'And *you* don't know me. I've put the fear of God into him. How long to Murmansk?'

Cameron said, 'Two days. You know we're bound for Murmansk, do you – not Archangel with the convoy?'

'Yes. I was told the score before I left the flagship. Two days . . . he should be fit enough by then, but he'll need to take it easy, Cameron.' Matthews started to turn away, then hesitated. 'His eyes. Have you ever noticed anything?'

Cameron had taken up his binoculars to make a sweep around the convoy, now reformed and steadied on its easterly course. 'Can't say I have really. He's been rubbing at them a lot and looking a bit red in the whites, but that applies to us all. Why?'

114

Matthews shrugged. 'Not to worry. Just a thought.' He turned away and went down the ladder. Cameron watched him moving along the upper deck, lurching and holding like grim death to the lifeline. He took a long time to pass out of sight. Cameron had not yet seen him unravelled from his wool cocoon and wondered whether his stripes of rank were straight or wavy. Wondering about stripes he thought of Fasher. Nothing much had been seen of the gunner during the action. On the face of it there seemed to have been a certain lack of zeal, which was not the sort of thing you associated with gunners, RN.

His mind switched again: Leading Seaman Holloway's body, currently being sewn into his hammock with weights at the feet, had to be seen overboard. That would be done during the afternoon watch, the enemy permitting. A letter would have to be written to the next-of-kin, but Hawkey would want to see to that, though 'want' was scarcely the word for a task no one liked. Amazingly, Holloway had been the only fatal casualty apart from the man who'd gone overboard. They'd been lucky; but it was regrettable that it had had to be Holloway. Holloway could have saved the ship for all Cameron knew. He would have a word with Hawkey and suggest a recommendation when the official report of the action went in. As soon as circumstances permitted, which would probably not be before they returned to Scapa, a messdeck auction would be held of all the dead men's gear for the benefit of their dependents. Holloway's would do well. Such auctions were one way in which a man's messmates could show their sympathy by bidding hard-earned pay ridiculously above the value of the articles on offer: five bob for a pair of scaly socks, a quid for a knife, that sort of thing. And Holloway had been a popular leading hand.

Below, Fasher also was thinking about Holloway. Fasher had passed most of the action looking busy whilst keeping as far for'ard as possible, utterly convinced that the stern was about to be blown sky high. He hadn't gone on to the fo'c'sle where he could be seen by that johnny-come-lately RNVR on the bridge and asked why he wasn't taking charge aft. He had

115

kept himself under the lee of the bridge superstructure, darting from port to starboard and back again efficiently but dead scared inside. Jutland was in his mind throughout; his stomach became loose. He'd had another worry too: Holloway. What Holloway had said . . . but now that worry was past. Things usually sorted themselves out and this time was no exception. Dead men told no tales. That afternoon while Cameron read the committal service Fasher listened respectfully, his hand raised to the salute as Holloway flopped from under the White Ensign and a crocodile-tear look on his face.

'He was a good killick,' he said to Cameron afterwards. 'I had a lot of time for Holloway.'

Cameron said drily, 'I'm glad to hear it, Guns,' and turned away before Fasher could see the look of dislike. Cameron had not forgotten the charge brought by the gunner. He had half a mind to dig a little deeper into the whys and wherefores of Fasher's absence from the depth charges when the ship was in danger, but decided not to. Not now, anyway; this wasn't the time for discord. That had to be up to Hawkey if he wished to raise it later, when he got to hear about it as he was bound to.

Soon after the next day's dawn, by which time the wind, though remaining icy cold, had moderated, the expected reinforcements from Archangel joined the convoy escort. Weatherby, now back to duty, made the obvious remark: they were a trifle late but would no doubt be welcome enough on the convoy's onward passage. To some extent they would replace the *Durham* and the lost destroyers and corvettes, also the reduction in the *Belfast*'s gun power. By this time, Tovey's ships had broken off and returned westwards to resume their watch over the Denmark Strait and the northern exits to the Atlantic where other vital convoys were on passage from the United States.

Soon after the escorts had joined, the expected signal came from the *Belfast*:

Sprinter from Flag, you are to detach on the executive and proceed independently in accordance with previous orders. Reports indicate Murmansk icing up earlier than usual and you should keep a careful watch for pack ice. Good luck go with you. Thank you for your support so far.

Cameron sent the acknowledgement and passed the word down to Hawkey. Ten minutes later the yeoman, his glass to his eye, reported, 'Executive, sir.'

'Thank you, Yeoman. Starboard ten.'

Weatherby repeated the order down the voice-pipe and *Sprinter* came round to head alone for Murmansk and whatever might await her. When she was on course and the convoy, or what was left of it, was starting to fade to the north-east, Cameron went below for a word with Hawkey. He was worried about the report of ice, but Hawkey, looking completely washed-out and as weak as a kitten, put his mind at rest. He said. 'They'll send out ice-breakers. You just follow in.'

'And getting out again, sir?'

'Same. Unless it thickens and even the ice-breakers can't make it.'

'Then we stay in through the winter?'

Hawkey said, 'Perhaps, but that's an extreme view. Though sometimes I feel I wouldn't really mind.' He closed his eyes. There was no talk now of going back to the bridge. Cameron reflected on what the Surgeon Lieutenant had said, or anyway hinted. About Hawkey's eyes . . . and Weatherby had said Hawkey had found everything red and distorted that day on the bridge when he'd almost collapsed from exhaustion. Cameron went thoughtfully back to the bridge and once again took up his endless vigil, feeling by now as though he was nothing better than an automaton.

Thirty-six hours later the lookouts raised the ice-breakers emerging from the port of Murmansk.

11

GRIM hills white with snow rose behind the lumbering, monstrous ice-breakers. The sky hung heavy, a pall of gloom and foreboding. Pack-ice lay all around, rumbling, creaking, groaning past the frigate's hull as Cameron conned her in through the path made for him by the Russian vessels. The crews of those ice-breakers, the first communists Cameron had ever seen apart from Marshal Yurigin, looked morose and unwelcoming, though a hand had waved from a wheelhouse when a signal had come in poor English telling him to follow. The whole area looked forbidding; there was a feeling that the British were useful enough but were not really wanted.

Able Seaman Dander, clearing away snow and chipped-off ice, leaned on his broom and scowled towards the vessels ahead. 'Shower o' bastards,' he said to Leading Seaman Trott.

'Why, Stripey?'

'Oh, I dunno . . . I keep thinking of 'Olloway. Don't suppose you follow.'

Trott said briskly, 'I reckon I do at that, but we're all in the same boat, risking our bloody necks for that lot. Off your broom, Stripey. Look British!'

Stripey said, 'Ah, bollocks, mate,' but got to work again. He'd swept his guts out this trip, swept and hammered at blocks of ice and swept again. More than a man should be expected to bear, it was. But maybe he'd get a run ashore in Murmansk and find himself a tart. Always supposing the bloody thing was still there and not snapped off like a perishing icicle. God knew, it was more than cold enough. Not long before, he'd met an old mate of his in Loch Ewe, off a destroyer on the Murmansk run. This bloke had told him he'd peed over the side from his action station once, and never again. He'd found himself joined to the hogwash by a streak of bloody ice . . . painful when it snapped off.

Hawkey had resumed the command after they had secured alongside. Able Seaman Parsons, acting as harbour quarter-master at the gangway, had just been told off by the Captain to send for Marshal Yurigin and Mr Harcourt Prynn when Hawkey called him again on the sound-powered telephone in the QM's lobby, this time wanting Mr Cameron and sounding stressed. Parsons, having already despatched the boatswain's mate on the first errand, went down himself. When he knocked, Cameron was dead asleep. It took him a while to come through the layers and as he did so he became aware of the urgency in Parsons' voice. He roused himself and sat up, rubbing at his eyes. Cold struck like a knife.

'What is it?' he asked thickly.

'Captain, sir. Wants you at once. I've just sent down for the passengers, too. There's a Captain Sykes there . . . come aboard half an hour ago.'

'Army or Navy?'

'Navy, sir. Four ringer RN. BNLO Murmansk. Seen him on previous runs.'

'All right, Parsons. Coming.'

Able Seaman Parsons left the cabin. He, too, was nearly out on his feet. Moving along the alleyway he all but bumped into the gunner. Fasher shoved him aside, into the bulkhead, without a word. Parsons turned and gave him a V-sign, sort of, behind his back. Sod Fasher. Holloway was gone but he, Parsons, wasn't. Fasher didn't know anything about that, didn't know what Parsons knew about him. Maybe he would if he didn't watch out. Fuming inside, Parsons went back to the quartermaster's lobby near the after brow and stared gloomily at Murmansk, what you could see of it through the snow. Talk about a blizzard; Scapa was often bad enough but

119

it had nothing on this. Parsons thanked God he wasn't a Russian. As Parsons ruminated and thought longingly about a nice hot cup of kye that he would soon muster an excuse to go and get from the galley, Cameron knocked at Hawkey's door and was bidden to enter. Cameron was introduced to Sykes; Harcourt Prynn and Marshal Yurigin looked dourly displeased. Sykes was obviously in a bad mood, and his handshake with Cameron was a perfunctory one. The reason soon became clear: Marshal Yurigin. Resuming an interrupted conversation Sykes said acidly, 'Your hosts did their best, Marshal.'

'You were not there.'

'No. But I know my service. And I know the sacrifice of life.'

'So little compared with the Russian armies opposing Hitler outside Stalingrad. So little –'

'Yes, yes, I'm aware of the Russian heroism. God knows I hear of little else in Murmansk –'

'That is rude.'

'It's also fact,' Sykes snapped, 'but I apologize, Marshal. I'd simply like a little recognition that the British are also taking their share – that's all.'

'We are glad of them,' Yurigin said reluctantly, evidently deciding that the hatchet should now be buried. 'I wish to know what are the arrangements made for me.'

'Yes.' Sykes cleared his throat. 'You'll be aware, of course, that the original intention was –'

'To land me at Archangel, yes, of course. But now I am in Murmansk.'

'Yes, quite. I'm sure you realize that the reason for all this is simply to confuse the enemy. I don't need to tell you that we have German agents in Murmansk as well as in Archangel – many of them are believed to be here but so far none of them have been blown. The Nazis will be expecting you and Mr Prynn to be landed in Archangel – that's if they've got on to your presence in the convoy and it's only prudent to assume they have. You'll appreciate that too –'

'Of course. And the arrangements?' Yurigin smashed a fist

into his palm. 'To Moscow we must get, this Harcourt Prynn and I.'

Sykes shook his head. He lowered his voice as he said, 'Not to Moscow, Marshal. To Belomorsk, in the Karelian Republic.'

'Why is this?' Yurigin, eyes wide, sat forward with his hands on his knees. 'Tell me why this is, please!'

Sykes said, 'Mr Molotov is there. I think I need not say more.'

'Molotov is not in Moscow?' Yurigin asked after a pause.

'No.'

'I see. And it is Comrade Molotov's order that I go to Belomorsk?'

Sykes nodded. 'That's right, Marshal.'

'Then to Belomorsk I go. The arrangements, please.'

Sykes exchanged a look with Hawkey. He said, 'It's been decided that the risks are too great for you and Mr Prynn to go as yourselves. You must be given cover.'

'I am in my own country. I do not agree.'

Sykes sighed; the sigh said that he had expected this and that he knew it was impolitic for a liaison officer to anger a Russian marshal inside Russia, but he had his duty to do nonetheless. He said, 'The decision has been taken, Marshal. Until you reach Belomorsk you're a British Naval responsibility, I'm afraid. I assure you this is not by our wish. As it is, we have had to make arrangements and Mr Molotov has himself approved our suggestions. It's all authenticated and all decided.'

Yurigin was not satisfied. 'I make the decisions for my own person in my own country,' he said angrily.

'Not this time. I'm sorry. But you'll be in good hands. Lieutenant Hawkey will give you the details – I have to be off.' Captain Sykes was anxious to escape before Yurigin began more protests and objections. He stood up and shrugged himself into a greatcoat with his stripes of rank on the shoulders, then covered this with an outsize duffel coat. He had no uniform cap; instead he carried a Russian fur cap with ear-flaps.

121

When Sykes had been saluted over the brow and had vanished into the falling snow along the dockside, Hawkey came back to his cabin to pass the orders for Belomorsk.

No shore leave was piped; and Stripey Dander wasn't the only member of the ship's company who thought sadly about Russian tarts and the possibilities that had been snatched away when their virtual imprisonment had been piped throughout the ship. *Why*, was the question. Able Seaman Parsons had the answer.

'The bloody passengers,' he said. 'Skipper doesn't want any slips, any trouble, stands to reason – can't blame him.' He grinned and lit a fag, blew smoke across the mess table. 'You know what we are. Go ashore, get pissed, be rude to the Russkies, start a fight. Doesn't help – draws attention, does trouble of that sort. It's not only the flippin' passengers, either. For our own good, this is, up to a point like. You don't want to get arrested in bleedin' Russia and end up diggin' salt in Siberia.'

'Better than the bloody convoys,' Dander said. Parsons told him not to be so wet. Tempers were always frayed at the end of a Russian convoy and Dander was older than Parsons by some years and felt the prestige of his three good-conduct stripes . . . you didn't have to go ashore to start a fight. It didn't really get under way: both Stripey Dander and Parsons were held back by their messmates, and just as well when Mr Fasher appeared from the galley flat with the gunner's mate and the buffer. Fasher ran an eye over the seamen, some standing, most of them sitting on the benches at the mess tables.

'On your feet when you see an officer,' the gunner's mate said for Fasher. Half mutinously, the sitters rose. The gunner's mate stabbed a finger in various directions. 'You an' you an' you,' he said. By the time he finished he had selected a dozen men. 'Right, get fell in along the upper deck, starboard side.' He turned to Fasher. 'All right, sir?'

Fasher nodded. 'They'll do.' He turned on his heel and stalked away followed by the two petty officers. There was no word as to what the party was supposed to be detailed for.

Parsons asked rhetorically, 'Now what's in the bloody wind?'

Hawkey had passed the orders. Cameron had been told to remain behind in the cabin with Harcourt Prynn and Marshal Yurigin when Captain Sykes had left the ship. Coming back, Hawkey lost no time. He still looked pinched and ill. He said, 'Well now, gentlemen. Belomorsk. I want you to be in charge of the escort, Cameron. Twelve seamen under a petty officer and a leading hand. And Mr Fasher. Mr Harcourt Prynn and Marshal Yurigin will travel incognito . . . dressed as British seamen.' Hawkey gave a rather wan smile. 'There's an element of melodrama, isn't there, but it's serious enough, Cameron, and I don't suppose I need to stress that.'

'No, sir.' Cameron didn't like it; both Prynn and Yurigin were too old in his view to look like genuine British seamen. This could well have been one of Churchill's bright ideas, misconceived but forced through against other people's better judgment: Prynn and Yurigin didn't like it either, and said so, but Hawkey told them that neither he nor they had any option in the matter.

'It's been decided at high level,' he said tiredly, 'and approved by Marshal Stalin. It's considered to be the best way of fooling the German agents. You'll travel by train to Belomorsk as a British Naval guard . . . officially you're representing the UK at a communist party rally, to show solidarity against the Nazis – something like that,' he added to Cameron. 'That's why Fasher's going. We have to be authentic and Fasher has the parade-ground stuff off pat, of course. Now, the details. Marshal Yurigin . . . there's some similarity of build between him and Able Seaman Dander. I suggest he wears Dander's uniform. Again in the interest of authenticity – the pretence that our passengers are still aboard for the time being – Dander will take over Marshal Yurigin's clothing.'

Cameron grinned to himself. Marshal Yurigin had many of the physical hallmarks of a three-badgeman – full-bodied

stomach, bloated face, gnarled hands and toughened skin –
and Dander's uniform would sit easily enough on him. But
the British drill! Cameron was relieved to learn that neither
Harcourt Prynn nor Marshal Yurigin wc"ld be required
actually to perform as members of the guard after arrival at
Belomorsk. The party would be met at the railway station by
Russian military transport and the erstwhile passengers
would be handed over. The genuine Naval party would then
march behind a Russian band to the rally to be held in the
main square.

When Stripey Dander was apprised by Cameron of his
role, he went pale. 'Stone the bleedin' crows, sir! Perishin'
sittin' duck for the Nazis! Why *me*, sir?'

'Same shape,' Cameron said crisply. 'You should think
yourself flattered. Besides, you'll be treated as a marshal of
the USSR for a day or two. That's better than the messdeck.
You'll have a cabin all to yourself.'

'Officer, eh.' Stripey considered the perks attendant upon
that elevation. Well, it was an ill wind . . . and anyway he
wasn't being given any option. Orders were orders. Stripey,
still in his seagoing rig of jersey and old, worn-out trousers
under overalls, scarves, gloves, duffel coat and anything else
that could be dragged on to keep out the Russian cold, went
to his locker and brought out his Number Three uniform, the
one with red badges, the gold of his Number Ones being too
good for a bolshie. It would be something to boast about
when he got back to Scapa, how his uniform had been worn
by a Russian marshal in the interest of winning the bloody
war, and himself lording it aft, being waited on hand and foot
by the officers. Cor! Some lark, that.

There was no time to be lost. The exchange of uniforms was
quickly made. Harcourt Prynn was fitted out by a leaner
member of the ship's company who, in the civilian apparel of
the Minister for War Production, joined Stripey Dander who
was wearing the smock discarded by Marshal Yurigin.
Dander was disappointed at not being arrayed in golden
splendour but recognized that at least he would be a less
glittering target for any Jerry snipers that might be lurking in

the dockyard when he took exercise on the quarterdeck. The two disguised ratings were in the galley flat and wondering when their duties would begin when Petty Officer Bremner came in to pass the word that as soon as the shore party had left, the ship would be shifted into dry-dock for temporary repairs to her bow plating and after superstructure. All hands would be piped shortly.

Stripey Dander put his nose in the air. 'That won't include us, Buff. Officers, like, now. Entitled to a salute, I am, from the likes o' you.'

Bremner gave Dander a long look. 'Officers my arse. You'll work part-of-ship when you're not play-acting – *if* I say. For now, you're excused duty.'

Stripey looked offended. He was thinking himself into his role and almost convincing himself that he'd had a real genuine leg-up. Loftily he said, 'Thank you for nothing. I 'ave me orders from the skipper.'

Bremner made a shoo-ing motion with his hands. 'Bugger off, Stripey, before you get a boot up the backside.'

Within half an hour of Hawkey passing the orders, the party had left the ship, marching in greatcoats, chin-stays down and side-arms dangling, rifles at the slope and right arms swinging as the gunner's mate called the step. He was moving up and down the flanks, a busy sheepdog. In rear marched Leading Seaman Trott. Ahead of the line of march was Mr Fasher, in his element, a sword-hilt sticking out from the gash in his greatcoat, the end of the sword just visible beneath the coat's bottom and tapping against his shiny black patent-leather gaiters. Ahead again was Cameron, similarly dressed with a sword borrowed from the Captain. Alongside Cameron was a sub-lieutenant sent by Sykes from the British Naval Liaison Office to act as guide as far as the railway station. In the centre of the files of seamen were Marshal Yurigin and Harcourt Prynn. Yurigin, as a soldier, marched impeccably; Prynn shambled, to the despair of the gunner's mate who, like all gunner's mates, couldn't abide slovenliness – besides, the stupid ha'porth would give himself away by his cackfootedness. Daft, the gunner's mate thought it was; no one in their senses would really have detailed a cross between a sack of potatoes and a lame camel for a ceremonial guard. He stuck close to Harcourt Prynn, hoping to shield him from at least one side. If some Jerry took a pot shot on the other, well, that would be just too bad.

They reached the station intact: no incidents as they'd battled through the snow. It was, in truth, more of a trudge than a march and there had been only a sprinkling of spectators, no good cover for a Nazi gunman. Any such, Cameron thought, would have been immediately rumbled by the very obvious OGPU thugs that he'd seen standing about at street corners, watching dourly. No one had raised a cheer, not so much as a wave even, though it would have been obvious they'd come from a convoy escort. All that frozen way, all those deaths, and not a murmur. Perhaps it was too cold even for the Russians. . .

They were met at the station by Captain Sykes, together with another man, a shark-faced Englishman wearing plain clothes. This man's name was not mentioned, but he walked up and down the windswept platform with Sykes and Cameron. Sykes, speaking with his coat collar turned up around his face, said in a low voice, 'You'll have to know the score, Cameron. You can pass it on to your gunner, but no one else.' He paused, eyes flickering to right and left. 'It's vital that Mr Prynn makes his contacts in Belomorsk, then later – depending on the military situation – in Moscow. There's a big deal in the air – increased supplies from UK on our part, some post-war guarantees on theirs. I can't go into details. Now, it's entirely genuine that Nazi agents are out to get Prynn and stop this deal going through – they want to gain time to allow Hitler to reach Moscow before the supplies are stepped up. But that's not our only concern. The other is Yurigin.'

'Yes, sir. I know the Nazis are out to get him as well.'

Sykes gave a bitter laugh. 'Yes. But not for the reasons you think, Cameron! Yurigin's changed his loyalties – or so I'm told.' He glanced sideways at his civilian companion; there

126

was no response. Sykes went on, 'The word reached Murmansk just ahead of the convoy. Something broke in Moscow as a result of telephone taps – things went wrong for Yurigin in his absence. He's said to believe Russia's losing the war on the Moscow front. He was in contact with Nazi agencies whilst in London, apparently – I don't vouch personally for the truth of any of this, of course, politics being the jungle it is – and he's intending to join them when he gets his chance. It seems he's not ready just yet, which is why he risked coming back into Russia. He needs to learn a little more to pass on. That's the story, at all events.'

Cameron was rocked. He asked, 'You mean he'll be arrested on arrival in Belomorsk, sir?'

Sykes said, 'That's another story and one I'm not associated with.' Once again he glanced at his companion and said quietly, 'Over to you, friend!'

The civilian said, 'If he gets there, he'll be arrested – yes. Actually, the Russians don't want him to get there. It's not considered good for the populace to know that one of their generals has lost heart and gone over to the enemy – I see the point, I must say.' The man paused; it was a lengthy silence. Then he said with a touch of impatience, 'I don't know if you get the drift? Some sort of accident. . . I'd prefer not to have to put it into words.'

127

12

THE train moved off in a cloud of steam and a heavy rattle of bumpers. The day had darkened further and the cold was more intense than ever. There was no heating whatsoever on the train and no availability of food: someone had slipped up, not unusually. In the expectation of provision having been made, no rations had been brought by the Naval party so hunger was going to be the order of the day. And thirst. One coach had been earmarked for the British, who didn't fill it, so there was at least room to move around. The rest of the train was taken up by goods wagons that mostly seemed to carry human freight stacked in like the cargo the wagons had been built for. There were two other passenger coaches filled with Russian officers and their families. Also some important-looking civilians. Cameron had watched them going into comfort, with heavy winter clothing and hampers of food. Some people did all right in Russia, even under war conditions; Russia wasn't all Stalingrad or Moscow, wasn't all blood and sacrifice and Siberia.

Harcourt Prynn sat next to Marshal Yurigin and facing them were Leading Seaman Trott and Able Seaman Parsons. In the next section along Cameron sat with Fasher, two alone with their dignity as officers. Harcourt Prynn, though of course he understood the circumstances, was ill at ease in his guise as an ordinary seaman. He had little enough in common with Yurigin and he had less with Trott and Parsons, who seemed to be enjoying themselves and talking of little else but sex and the rotten quality of the beer to be had in the canteen at Lyness in Scapa. That, and what they looked forward to doing on their next boiler-cleaning leave, which again was concerned with sex and drink. Harcourt Prynn gathered, unwillingly enough, that the only time an effing ship's company got effing leave was when it was effing boiler-cleaning in an effing civilized port and the effing dockyard mateys took over.

Harcourt Prynn tried to shut his ears to it and pretended to be snoozing. He wondered what sailors would do without that particular four-letter word. They would barely be able to speak. His mind drifted. In happier times when the world had been at peace, Harcourt Prynn and his wife had been participants in an interesting hobby. When they went on holiday, they stayed in hotels and afterwards they complained about them to anyone who cared to listen, first their own family and next people they met at cocktail parties or silver weddings or receptions or what-have-you. *Never stay at so-and-so, it's perfectly frightful. There isn't a single good hotel in the whole of Yorkshire. The last place we stayed at was worse than the one before, and that's saying something.* The worse the hotel the more the Harcourt Prynns enjoyed their holiday, because the more there was to talk about afterwards. They did their talking in despairing tones and with uplifted noses and eyeballs that rolled beseechingly to heaven. As time went on, they unconsciously began to pick the hotels they knew they would complain about when they got back. They would find no joy whatever in staying in a complaint-proof hotel. It was well worth the money to be commiserated with afterwards. They never found out what bores they were.

Harcourt Prynn was now thinking that all those carefully-nurtured complaints must sometimes have sounded a little hollow. Since embarking aboard that horrible frigate, he had met real life. And as for this dreadful jolting train with no food or hope of food, and no heat. . .

'Well, sod me,' came the voice of Leading Seaman Trott, returning with a clatter of equipment from a walk up and down the coach, 'there don't even seem to be any effing heads aboard. . .' There then came the sound of a window being opened, followed by a pause. Harcourt Prynn opened his eyes and shut them again quick. How disgusting, he thought, I'd sooner burst than do that.

Cameron sat rigid in his seat, going over and over Sykes' words and the civilian's final devastating hint. He had said nothing to Fasher yet, even though he'd had the okay to do so. First he had to sort out his own mind. The hint had been simple enough: Yurigin was to be lost en route, left to take a Nazi bullet if an attack should come. Be shoved into the line of fire, in fact; and, failing an attack, an 'accident' was to be contrived, some phoney panic – something of that sort. But Cameron wasn't prepared to kill a man in cold blood. Yurigin hadn't done him any harm, and he'd behaved well in the matter of Holloway. Cameron detested being thrust into an involvement in politics, which he knew this to be. It wasn't his job as a Naval officer, as a seaman. And why couldn't it have been done in Murmansk if it had to be done at all? Yurigin could have been sent packing off the ship to take his chance against the OGPU. Not that he would have had one, of course – if the suspicions were correct. Simple! But there were always the wheels within wheels and for some reason this method must have suited Comrade Stalin better.

It was a very dirty business.

Indeed it was: behind Cameron, Marshal Yurigin – in whose mind, in actual fact, no thoughts of disloyalty lay – was growing apprehensive about his forthcoming meeting in Belomorsk. Why Molotov – why not Stalin, in Moscow as intended? It was a worry to a Russian; Yurigin knew his Russia and he knew his leader as well. Change, sudden alterations of orders for no real reason that had been divulged, never boded good for a high-ranking officer of the military. And Stalin . . . the generalissimo was, as Yurigin had reflected often enough, a difficult man and one of extreme temper, far from predictable. He was also, though Yurigin recognized the danger of such a thought, a man of spilt blood. There had been pogroms, slaughter of political opponents, banishments to the dread Siberian salt mines. And Marshal Yurigin was uneasy for other reasons than the

130

altered arrangements for the meeting; there had been straws in the wind that had indicated to him that Stalin had little personal liking for him, that the great leader was perhaps jealous of him and of the way in which he had been feted as much as wartime Britain would permit. Stalin had a short way with people whom he didn't like, people who might get in his way. Always a highly-placed officer had to step with care in case Comrade Stalin was given the impression that that officer might have designs upon his own position. Marshal Yurigin reflected, but kept such thoughts from his expression as he gazed from the train windows at the snows of his homeland, that in some matters there was little difference between Stalin and the abominable Adolf Hitler.

And there was something curious about the way in which he was being taken to Belomorsk: it was almost as though he were under escort. Fear was creeping slowly into Yurigin as the train made its slow progress south, its great snow-shares casting the thick fall from the track as it went. Aboard the British frigate he had had that other reflection – that Stalin would be furious at the loss of war material should the convoy come under severe attack and would take out his anger on his floating marshal in some way. By now, for certain, Stalin would have heard that most of the convoy's cargo had gone to the bottom. Stalin would rant and rave at the British via their ambassador and any admirals with whom he came into contact, but that was all he could do to them, and, as Yurigin reminded himself once again, Stalin dearly loved a scape-goat. . .

There was something in the air. A threat.

Yurigin glanced sideways at Harcourt Prynn. There would be no help there. Prynn was in pawn to Churchill, and Churchill wished a spurious friendship with Comrade Stalin, a wartime marriage of convenience. He looked at Leading Seaman Trott and Able Seaman Parsons. If he really were under escort on Stalin's order those two would do their duty, and their duty would be dictated by their officer sitting behind him with the other officer, the one who had wished him to say that one of the British seamen had struck him. From that

131

officer no help would come either. But the other, the young man with the two wavy gold stripes, he looked honest and trustworthy and humane, and he was the one in charge.

Marshal Yurigin, like Harcourt Prynn, had seen Leading Seaman Trott urinating from the train window, and now the memory gave him an idea.

Fasher said, 'This is a bloody lark, Mr Cameron, I don't think! Sooner we're back aboard the better I'll like it.' The gunner looked as though he half expected arrest by the OGPU at any moment and undoubtedly there was an unease about this penetration into the Russian land mass, a feeling that came from the fact of being cut off from all familiarity, the sea and the ship. The basic treachery – as Cameron saw it – of their mission made it so much the worse.

Responding to the gunner he said, 'Same here,' and he said it with sincerity. So far he had still not passed the orders to Fasher. Every now and again the train was stopping, held up by the snow until gangs went down to clear the blockage in front of the snow-share blades. When it moved, it moved slowly and there was not a lot of sound to overlay conversation. The men were not talking much either; the feeling of oppression had invaded their minds and had gradually overcome even the easy ribaldry of Naval ratings, their ability to joke and natter their way through most wartime situations.

'I don't like it at all,' Fasher said suddenly. 'Why isn't that bloke Yurigin being given a *military* escort, a Russian one, against the bloody Nazi agents, eh?'

'Reasons,' Cameron said shortly in a low voice. 'Good ones – I suppose.'

'Eh?'

Cameron leaned across towards the gunner; the time had come or Fasher's loud voice would arouse too much interest. Fasher, seeing what was wanted, also leaned close. Cameron said, 'We keep our voices low, all right? Listen carefully, Guns.' In as few words as possible he told Fasher what Sykes and the civilian had said back in the railway station. He added, 'I don't like it. I don't suppose you do either. I don't know what to do about it.'

He felt better, having told Fasher the facts. This could now be shared. But he didn't like Fasher's response even though he knew it was both correct and inevitable. Fasher said, 'Orders is orders. Not for us to question 'em.'

Cameron said steadily, 'The unspoken order was for him to be killed. Just that.'

'Most armies shoot bloody traitors.'

'Their own. We don't do it for them.'

Fasher shrugged. 'I don't know much about Yurigin. Maybe he's a popular general. Better for us to get the dirty end than Stalin.'

'And afterwards?'

'Afterwards?'

Cameron said, 'If he's so popular, what's the mob's reaction going to be when we get back to Murmansk?'

Fasher brought out a handkerchief and blew his nose. Then he said, 'Now look, Mr Cameron. You don't know the Navy yet . . . not properly, not like I do. I've been in a lifetime, from boy up. They won't see us get ripped apart, that'll all have been gone into, planned for, see? We'll have done our duty and knocked off one of bloody Hitler's men plonked right at the seat of Kremlin power. That's *got* to be good for the total Allied war effort, right? The way I see it, there's likely to be an attack from these Nazi agents. That's when Yurigin gets it.' He paused, then added, 'From *us*.'

There was something not far short of a look of anticipation in Fasher's face. It sickened Cameron. He said, 'I'm not going to do it, Guns.'

'Disobey orders, eh?'

'Up to a point. I'm going to find a way of letting him vanish. Then it's up to the Russians.'

'It's still disobedience of orders.'

'I'll take that chance,' Cameron said with finality. 'But I'm giving you the opportunity of – of dissociating yourself if you wish to, Guns.'

Fasher nodded, and turned his face towards the window,

hiding his expression from Cameron. He'd said his say and he wasn't going to say any more, not him. But it looked very much as though the cocky young bastard had handed it to him on a plate.

Yurigin got to his feet as once again the train stopped, this time at a station as he'd known it soon would. It wasn't much of a place and there was almost nothing of station buildings, but that didn't matter. He moved out from his seat and walked around its back to where Cameron was sitting. He noted the sudden caution in the eyes of both the British officers and this confirmed something. He recognized the look of the gaoler. It was an international, world-wide look.

He said, 'I leave the train. Just for a while.'

It was the other man who answered, the evil one. 'What for, Marshal, may I ask?'

'Natural purposes. There is no lavatory on the train. Near me, one man used the open window. I am a marshal of the USSR. I do not use windows.'

He turned away. Cameron put out a hand and said, 'Just a moment, sir. There could be danger. You must have an escort.'

'An escort, to relieve myself? I do not think so! Yet I understand your point and your situation. You are responsible. You shall come with me yourself. As a high-ranking officer I am entitled to ask this.'

Cameron nodded and got to his feet. He wondered if Yurigin had tumbled to the facts; the Russian had spoken as though he realized he was under guard for more than his physical safety against German agents. Cameron gestured towards the door and said, 'After you, sir.' Then he caught Fasher's eye; the gunner's face was blank but the eye said that Fasher knew the moment had come. Fasher, however, didn't interfere. Yurigin pushed open the door and dropped down to the track, agilely for a man of his years. Cameron followed.

Yurigin moved away from the train. He said, 'I must speak to you. It is important. But first, the call of nature is genuine and must be obeyed.' Full night had fallen by this time; the

134

Russian moved away into the shadows. Cameron, glancing back at the train, saw Fasher get to his feet and stand in the open doorway. Cameron found himself praying that Yurigin would make a dash for it; but he didn't. He came back.

Yurigin said, 'You will tell me the truth, please. I am entitled to know. I am in your hands. I am a man of honour. I shall respect your confidence.'

This was a tough one; it had been inherent in all that had been said on the platform at Murmansk that Yurigin was not to know of the suspicions. If the fact had not been stated in so many words, then it had certainly been as it were signalled in cypher. Like Nelson, Cameron wasn't going to see the signal; he came out with it bluntly. He said, 'I'm told you're believed to have had dealings with the Nazis, sir.'

'No! I, Marshal Yurigin?' The man was rocked, there was no doubt at all about that. But he was in control of himself. He said, 'No, this is not so. It is all lies! I love Russia and have fought for her in the field, and will do so again. This is far from the truth, though there are those who will make it appear to be the truth and more lies will be told.' Yurigin turned away and paced up and down in extreme agitation for a while, then came back and faced Cameron. Cameron found the ring of sincerity in what Yurigin had said; and, come to think of it, Sykes hadn't appeared all that convinced of the suddenly announced suspicions . . . Yurigin said, 'I think this is what you in your country would call a frame. I can explain it in no other way, but I ask you to believe what I say.'

Cameron asked, 'Do you believe that certain persons are using an excuse . . . finding a reason, a false one, to discredit you?'

Yurigin gave a sad, tired smile. He said, 'You are a forthright young man, but yes, that is what I believe. I think so, yes.'

Cameron nodded. Without pausing to reflect further, he said, 'You're free to go, Marshal Yurigin. You're familiar with this part of Russia?'

'Yes –'

'Then you'll make out. You'll find people who'll help,

135

people who know your loyalty?'

Yurigin nodded. 'Yes. But you, my good young man? You will have lost your prisoner. What will happen to you?'

'That's my worry, sir,' Cameron said. 'All I ask is that you appear to break away – have a go at me, knock me for six. You agree?'

Cameron didn't know whether or not Yurigin would have run; there was something in his face, clear in the light from the train windows, that said he would be unwilling to allow a young officer to jeopardize his future. He could also be thinking that to break away might go against him; possibly he would prefer to face his accusers and fight back. But something intervened before he reached a decision and that something was Fasher. Fasher jumped down from the train, leaping from the open door with a service revolver in his hand.

'I heard all that,' he said loudly. 'Marshal Yurigin, you'll kindly nip back aboard, pronto, or I'll shoot you for a bloody traitor. And the same goes for you, *Mister* Cameron.'

13

By now none of the Naval party was in any doubt as to what appeared to be the facts: the Russian was a lousy traitor due for the high jump and Mr Cameron had tried to aid and abet his escape from his proper fate. He'd been stopped by Fasher. And Fasher was now in charge and not listening to a word Cameron tried to say. Fasher still had his revolver out and was sitting opposite Yurigin and Cameron as the train moved off south again. Fasher had both of them covered.

It was an unprecedented situation and every man was agog to see what happened next. You didn't often see a commissioned officer arrested by a warrant officer, nor did you see a marshal of the USSR in the same situation.

Opinions were divided, and expressed *sotto voce*. Most were for Cameron simply because they loathed Fasher's guts and hated to see him come out on top. And they liked Cameron; he was a decent bloke and he'd done well throughout the convoy. He didn't shirk action, not like Fasher, whose disappearance from aft when the depth charges looked like going up was now a subject of comment among all hands. But none of them knew of Yurigin's protestations of innocence because Fasher hadn't said anything about that, and that part hadn't been overheard by anyone other than Fasher, and Yurigin, having had his say, wasn't adding anything further. He looked not defeated exactly, but resigned. There was no sympathy for Yurigin, who had sounded arrogant when he'd said, in effect anyway, that he was going for a pee and had been overheard to say or at any rate imply that a high-ranking officer shouldn't be expected to pee in front of ratings; that was hardly a Bolshie sentiment – much more Nazi. And, of course, there was no doubt about the fact that Cameron shouldn't have tried to let the bugger go free.

There was just one man who knew beyond any doubt that Fasher was a bloody liar and that he couldn't be relied on: Able Seaman Parsons, who still had Holloway very much in mind. Fasher had an Achilles heel that could finish him off, and when the time came Parsons was going to bash that heel for six. And whatever the rights and wrongs of wanting to let a traitor go, Parsons hoped that when he opened his mouth, Cameron would be let out from under.

There was another stop further on and this time such of the party as had been too bashful to use the windows, not many of them, got down on to the track to relieve themselves. From further up the train, some Russian women got down on a similar errand and vanished into the night beyond the rim of light from the train. There was some laughter and low comment. Cameron got to his feet and said he was going down to the track.

Fasher said, 'You're not, you know.'

'I've got to. Come if you like.'

'And leave him?' Fasher gestured with his revolver at Yurigin. 'Let it boil.'

Cameron said, 'The party's armed in case you've forgotten. Call up one of the hands.' After that he didn't wait; he opened the door and got down to the track. Fasher sat for a moment, his face twisted. Then he got up.

'You,' he said.

Able Seaman Parsons stared at him. 'Yes, sir?'

'Take your rifle, go and watch Mr Cameron. And stamp out that cigarette.'

Very deliberately, Parsons dropped a butt-end on the floor of the coach and trod on it. Fasher said, 'Right, now get going before it's too late.'

'Get stuffed,' Parsons said.

138

Fasher's face went a deep red. 'Trouble-maker, eh? I've had my eye on you before. What's your name?'

'Parsons.'

'I'll give you one more chance, Parsons. Are you going to obey my order?'

Parsons said, 'No, I'm not.'

Fasher turned to Leading Seaman Trott. 'You heard that. Direct disobedience –'

'Bit deaf in that ear, sir.'

Fasher glared stonily. 'Which ear?'

'Both ears, sir. Didn't hear a thing.' Trott clambered to his feet and looked along the coach. There was a tense silence now. 'None o' you lads heard anything, did you?'

There was a chorus of virtuous negatives. But Fasher wasn't giving in yet. He spoke to Harcourt Prynn, whose face was turned to the window and the whiteness that seemed to lead to eternity. Fasher said, 'Mr Prynn, sir. You heard, I reckon. You haven't got cloth ears, have you?' There was almost a note of pleading in his voice. But Harcourt Prynn's eyes were closed and he was breathing a little heavily in assumed sleep. He was a minister of the Crown and as such must not become involved in disputes. Especially inside Russia with a delicate mission to carry out, the more delicate now because of the unexpected fracas over Marshal Yurigin. Things were bad enough already; and besides, the seamen looked a ruffianly lot and appeared to be on the verge of mutiny. He could be attacked if he took sides; the man Fasher looked and sounded quite beside himself and he carried a loaded revolver. It wouldn't be safe even to side with the majority. So Harcourt Prynn remained asleep and Fasher took the hint.

Trembling like a leaf, Fasher lifted his revolver. As he did so Cameron came back into the coach. Startled at what he saw developing, he left the door open behind him. All eyes were now on Fasher, who turned his head when he heard Cameron's entry. Then there was another sound: fast footsteps along the track. A hand appeared as a man heaved himself up into the coach. Two more men entered behind

139

him, and all carried sub-machine-guns. They were in OGPU uniforms but when they spoke it was in English and the accent was German.

Back in Murmansk Stripey Dander was reclining at his ease in the cabin allocated to Marshal Yurigin. He still wore the marshal's peasant smock. Peasant it might be, but ever since the passengers had embarked it had represented Soviet authority and Stripey didn't want to take it off even to turn in, which he intended doing shortly. He was so tired he was starting to drop off in his chair but he didn't want to waste grandeur in sleep. In the opinion of the ship's company Stripey was a good old bloke even if he did swing the lead whenever possible, and he was regarded as something of a character, so they'd played up. Most of them, anyway; the buffer was inclined to be a little tetchy when Stripey tried to come the marshal over him. Even bloody marshals, Bremner had said, had to obey someone's orders and this marshal was going to obey his. The first order, deriving from the skipper, was that the marshal had to stay below decks after pipe down. Having disported himself with a cigar on the quarterdeck in daylight, just as propaganda if any Jerry agents should be using their field glasses on the ship from the surrounding hills, he must act as prudently as any other marshal in the circumstances and stay where he was safe. Anyway, buffer or no buffer, a marshal couldn't be seen actually working around the decks so Stripey had got out of the business of shifting berth into the dry-dock.

Now he sat back in his nice, comfortable chair, legs out-thrust, feeling sorry for the lads in the dreary surround-ings of the messdecks. Marshals filled his roving fantasies: he sent common soldiers scurrying to fulfil his wishes, which were mostly concerned not with the conduct of Moscow's defence but with frothing glasses of beer plus a good supply of fags – tailor-made ones, not ticklers' roll-your-own. And girls with not much on. *All the nice girls love a marshal, all the nice girls love a Com. . .*

Stripey grinned to himself. What a bleeding lark . . . may

as well make the most of it while he could, it wasn't going to last beyond the time Mr Cameron got back from Belomorsk. He emerged from the cabin and yelled out, peremptorily, then went back in. In due course the officers' servant came along and stuck his face round the door curtain.

'What is it, Stripey?'

'Whisky, my good man,' Stripey said in the lofty tones of an officer and a gentleman. 'Chop-chop, too.'

'Stuff it, Stripey –'

'Now look 'ere –'

'I 'ave not', the officers' servant said haughtily and with finality, 'bin authorized to start a wine account in your name, so like I said, you can stuff it.'

Stripey was about to tell the man what he thought of him when there was a sound from along the alleyway, someone blundering about off the bulkheads it seemed to be. Stripey's eyes widened and he thought with a rush of terror about Jerry agents. But it wasn't that. He heard the skipper's voice, urgent, desperately worried about something – even frightened. The skipper was calling the steward, who swung round.

'Yessir, coming, sir.'

'I can't see,' Hawkey said in a strained voice. 'I can't see a thing. It's all . . . dark red. Get the doctor.'

Under the weaving snouts of the sub-machine-guns the Naval party was herded to the back end of the coach. The German spokesman ordered them to pass their rifles and side arms to the front. The order was obeyed and the rifles and bayonets together with Cameron's and Fasher's revolvers were piled in a heap between the British party and the men in the OGPU uniforms. Cameron and Fasher were the first in the line of fire.

'Who is in charge?' the German asked.

Cameron said, 'I am.' There was no argument about that from Fasher.

'I want Marshal Yurigin and your cabinet minister, Prynn. Which are they?' Sharp eyes peered. Cameron said the party was simply a ceremonial Naval guard en route for Belomorsk.

141

The Nazis took no notice, just pushed past, looking at faces, not in the least fooled by the ratings' uniforms. It took little time to find Marshal Yurigin. Indeed the Russian identified himself even before he was recognized.

He said quietly, 'I am Marshal Yurigin.'

That, Cameron thought, was self-sacrificial: Yurigin had acted to save shooting in which British lives would have been lost. Fasher looked at it differently; he said in a grating voice, 'That settles it, doesn't it, eh? This is his way of getting himself safely into Jerry hands.'

Cameron said, 'Mr Fasher, you're a bastard and a disgrace to your uniform.'

Fasher seemed about to make some reply when suddenly there was a series of shots from the front of the train, and on the heels of them, as one of the Germans made for the door, the train gave a heavy jerk, followed by more as the coach bumpers clashed together. The man at the door fell in a heap and the spokesman staggered backwards, his gun lifting. Yurigin was on him in a flash, and the two rolled over and over. The train gathered speed, slowly at first, then faster. Cameron moved fast towards the fighting men but as he did so the shooting started from the other two. Woodwork splintered, the air was filled with the acrid stench of gunsmoke. Three of the Naval party went down. Fasher took shelter behind a seat back; Harcourt Prynn stuffed his fingers into his ears and gave a yelping sound as he cringed on the floor and rolled himself up like a hedgehog. Cameron grabbed a rifle from the abandoned heap and used it as a club, dodging to right and left as bullets zipped close. A lucky swipe took one of the OGPU-uniformed men on the side of the head and he crashed like a log with blood pouring. Then the man grappling with Yurigin got the better of the ageing Russian; he slammed a fist into his jaw and got to his feet as Yurigin went out like a light. Cameron lost his grip on the rifle when the butt swung hard into the back of a seat. The third Nazi was firing from the hip to keep the Naval ratings back. More had gone down; Leading Seaman Trott lay dead, his lungs colandered. Yurigin's assailant clobbered Cameron as he

142

tried to fight back, and he went down with a heavy blow to the head.

He didn't hear Fasher's voice; Fasher had seen him fall and took his opportunity. He called out, 'All right, I'm in charge. We surrender.' He paused. 'That's Mr Harcourt Prynn, down there.'

The Surgeon Lieutenant was deeply sympathetic but there was nothing he could do. He said, 'I'm not an eye specialist, old chap. I know that's cold comfort but it's no use pretending. What I mean is, there's nothing I can actually do, beyond getting you to bathe the eyes – salt and water can't do any harm till we get you to a specialist.'

'A Russian one?'

'I shall try, certainly. If not, then we'll have to get you down to Rosyth when we get back to Scapa. I wouldn't worry too much in the meantime,' the doctor added cheerfully.

'It's not *your* eyes, damn you.'

'I know, I know. And I'm really terribly sorry. It's rotten luck.'

There was a pause. Then Hawkey said in a too-controlled voice, 'Sorry I snapped. I realize your position. Just tell me what the prognosis is, will you? Will my sight come back?'

'Oh, I should think so,' the doctor said brightly. 'It's very probably just temporary. It's rest you need now.'

Hawkey nodded miserably. His eyes hurt a lot, stinging like buggery was how he put it, and the red murk was horrible and frustrating. He had, somehow, to talk and go on talking, he didn't know why. He knew he was tending to babble. He said, 'This may sound stupid at my age, but I'm worried for my mother's sake.'

'That's not stupid.'

'You see, she's always wanted to see me fly my flag one day. After my brother went, that was. I was never all that keen. As a matter of fact I detest the bloody service. But that was what my mother wanted to see. She'll be able to see a flag all right, but it won't be mine. And there's so much to see, isn't there?'

The doctor murmured, 'Do try not to worry.'

'Even Scapa. Those sunrises when the weather's fair. God, I've often cursed them because it meant the Jerry submarines would be out on the next convoy! Now I'll never see them again.'

'Of course you will,' the doctor said, but although he did his best to sound convincing he heard his own insincerity creeping through because he knew that Hawkey believed his sight would never come back and his professional view happened to be that Hawkey was right.

He left the cabin, and went to mix up some salt with a little water. Bloody useless but you had to do something. Savagely, he cursed the war and the terrible havoc it was making of men's lives. In a few years' time all the sacrifices would be forgotten in the run-up to the next lot, or if that didn't come, then an uncaring generation would take over. The doctor wondered if, after it was all finished, they would carry on with poppy day. If they did, it would be so bloody ironic! And take the world ahead thirty or forty years, which wasn't all that long in terms of man's progress from the apes, and sod-all buyers would be found anyway.

The train rattled and lurched on for Belomorsk. The Russians had regained control of the engine but the Nazis were the masters in the coach. When he'd come round Cameron had been presented with the *fait accompli* of Fasher's surrender. He remembered he'd called Fasher a bastard and a disgrace to the service or something. That was unofficer-like language from one officer to another in front of ratings, but Cameron had no regrets, especially after he'd seen Harcourt Prynn isolated at the front of the coach, under guard with Yurigin, and he'd asked how come.

Yurigin told him. The Russian lifted a hand and pointed at Fasher. 'Him,' he said with contempt.

'You, Mr Fasher?'

Fasher snarled back. 'Yes, me, Mr Cameron. It had to come out sooner or later, there'd have been more killing else.'

Well, of course that was true. But Cameron made a guess

144

that Fasher hadn't lingered very long with the information. Meanwhile the Germans hadn't won out yet and they knew it. The train wasn't going to stop en route again now: next stop Belomorsk and a Russian welcome. Logically, the Germans had had it. Yet they might get away with it. It could be assumed they all spoke fluent Russian or they wouldn't have been sent in. Likewise they would know Russian military and secret police procedures, word perfect. They would also be aware of the set-up in Belomorsk, the names of the military commanders and high civilian officials. All that would help to make any subterfuge successful, or at least give it a good chance. Official OGPU uniforms and much loud voice-work could bring about miracles. Cameron tried to think himself into the German minds. What would they, or what could they, do on arrival?

Spin a yarn that they were acting under precise orders received from Stalin in Moscow, that they had arrested the traitor that Yurigin was officially said to be, and were charged now with his removal to a place of security until the decision of the Russian leadership was known? Then hustle the unfortunate marshal away, out into the countryside – they might even push it as far as demanding transport – and then get themselves over the frontier into Norway with their victims? It was all too possible. It was also more than likely that communication with embattled Moscow was disrupted and they would have a fine start.

There would, of course, be snags. Both Yurigin and Harcourt Prynn would need to be incommunicado. How could that be brought about without something showing? And there was the Naval party. None of them was going to stand silently by, which must be obvious enough to the German agents. Those ostensible OGPU gunmen might be in charge inside the coach; but they certainly hadn't intended being rushed willy-nilly into Belomorsk aboard the train. Yurigin and Prynn had been intended, surely, to have been hooked away at that last station, where transport could be presumed to have been waiting.

Cameron remembered that further back in the train there

had been Russian officers with their families, embarking like themselves in Murmansk. If only he could find a way of contacting them . . . the train was, unfortunately, not a corridor one. Each coach was separate. Some of those officers had been in OGPU uniforms: very likely they had been the disguised Germans now present, and had simply left their coach when the train stopped at the station and walked along the platform. But there would be others, genuine military officers and officials. Cameron had noticed that a wide step ran along each coach beneath the doors. It might be possible, if highly dangerous, just so long as he could get a door open. After that, the bullets; but the disarmed Naval guard could be relied on to tick over and start something that would give him time. There were still eight men left, plus the gunner's mate. And Fasher. Fasher was sitting alongside him. The Nazi agents were in a bunch, staring down the coach, ready behind the sub-machine-guns. The one who had been knocked out by the rifle butt was on his feet again. Cameron bent and fiddled with the fastening of his gaiters. Then, in a low voice, he spoke to Fasher.

'I'm going to try to reach the rear coaches,' he said. 'Those Russian officers . . . once they're alerted they can get out fast at Belomorsk and give the alarm.'

Fasher didn't respond and Cameron couldn't be sure he'd heard. Straightening, Cameron saw the gunmen looking directly towards him. And towards Fasher, which probably accounted for the silence. Then Fasher said loudly, 'Stupid bastard. Get us all shot.' There were two things in his voice: vituperous hate, and panic. His words hadn't been intended as a diversion; they'd been a plain warning to the Germans and a personal safeguard – Fasher was dissociating himself, the good untroublesome prisoner who would co-operate. Nevertheless, his words did cause a diversion of a sort and as one of the gunmen moved forward Cameron took advantage of it.

14

Captain Sykes in Murmansk had pulled a string or two, wishing the *Sprinter*'s men to have a touch of comfort whilst in transit after the rigours of the convoy; he had secured a coach of a type normally reserved for the Russian élite. The seats had cushions. As Cameron got swiftly to his feet he brought his cushion up with him and swung it hard at the advancing German's sub-machine-gun. The snout went down and bullets zipped into the floor. The German, taken off guard, plunged forward and almost fell. By this time Cameron had flung the door open and was out on the step, moving as fast as possible towards the rear of the train. A rush of freezing air tore at him and snow fell heavily. At the door a man appeared and bullets whistled past Cameron, close, ripping along the thick cloth of his uniform greatcoat. He didn't look behind: his whole attention was concentrated the way he was going. His hands grasped desperately at the door handles as he moved along the swaying train. Inside the coach before he reached its end he could see the enemy agents moving along, obviously to cut him off by opening another door. They were being impeded by the Naval ratings: all hell had been let loose and Cameron saw, fleetingly, one of the weapons being wrenched from a German hand. Then, and just in time as it happened, he reached the end of the coach. As more bullets ripped past him he looked back and saw two things: a man coming along in pursuit, and the frightening glimpse, the loom through the snow and the darkness of a tunnel wall materializing. He gave a shout of near panic; then he was able to drag himself in

147

between the two coaches, a comparatively safe position above the weaving buffers. As he did so he heard a high scream of blind terror and a moment later felt wetness on his face. Fragments of human wreckage came past. The man had been squashed like an insect.

It was a long tunnel; there could be others. He gritted his teeth and moved on again as the train came clear.

Able Seaman Parsons was watching Fasher's face. In the rearranged coach he was now sitting opposite the gunner. Only one more rating had died: the one Cameron had seen trying to get a grip on the sub-machine-gun. That had been an abortive attempt and the man, an OD on his first convoy, had been shot through the throat. After that, a cleaning-up operation had been mounted and Fasher had been the only one who had assisted the Jerries. All the bodies had been chucked out of the train to lie in disarray along the track. The Nazis didn't want to arrive at Belomorsk with bodies. The disposal made, they dealt with the blood as best they could. It was still a fair mess but they had to put up with it. The Jerries then told Fasher what they wanted of him and the others, and Fasher went along with them. Although Parsons didn't know this, the Jerries' plans, hastily reformulated, ran along much the same lines as Cameron's earlier thoughts. It was all to be done by bluff with a full display of high-handedness. People didn't often question the OGPU any more than they did the Gestapo, and the Jerries were Gestapo trained and fully confident. On arrival Fasher was to leave the train by himself and report a change of orders received in Murmansk: OGPU officers had taken over Marshal Yurigin and the British minister on direct instructions from the Kremlin and Fasher was to ask for transport to come alongside the coach and take off the OGPU men with their VIP charges. Fasher would be covered by the sub-machine-guns throughout and if there was any threatening move towards the train he would die instantly. When the arrangements had been made Fasher was to return to the train to await the transport and would then leave with the supposed OGPU men and the remainder of the

148

Naval party plus Yurigin and Harcourt Prynn. Thenceforward the British would be prisoners-of-war and once into Germany would be treated strictly in accordance with the Geneva Convention.

Some bloody hope, Parsons thought. They would all be shot when it was safe to do so and left to rot in the Russian backwoods while the Jerries beat it for the frontier. Or more likely a pick-up by aircraft in some pre-arranged spot inside Russia.

It could work for the Nazis. But a lot was going to depend on Fasher: Fasher, who didn't like the guns and would do his level best for his own skin. Maybe the thought of a later shooting had penetrated but Fasher wouldn't take chances on the certainty of immediate death if he failed the Nazis. Parsons believed all concerned would have a better chance if Fasher did fail, because then the Russians would storm the train. As for Mr Cameron, Parsons believed he'd most likely had it when one of the Jerries had been minced up by the tunnel wall. He was more than sorry about that; but now they had to act for themselves.

Fasher could yet be susceptible to pressure. If Parsons used a lever Fasher might very well have second thoughts. Fasher wasn't entirely a jelly; it took some considerable effort and intelligence to make gunner even if, in Fasher's case, a lot of dirty work had gone into it as well.

But it was worth a try.

Parsons said, 'You seem to have forgotten, but we've met before. Sir.'

'*Have* we. I've met many people. I'm not interested.'

'I believe you will be,' Parsons said. He looked at the men in the OGPU uniforms. They were watching but they didn't appear to mind a bit of conversation; they spoke English and Parsons' words were innocuous enough, even to Fasher. Parsons went on, 'It was some years ago as a matter of fact. Just one more poor bloody matloe you'd run in, got him detention – ninety days. You won't have forgotten the charge, Fasher.'

Fasher looked sideways. 'Parsons, isn't it? Remind me.

149

The name doesn't mean a thing.'

'I wasn't called Parsons then. It's a long story, Fasher, but I changed my name by deed poll. When my mum married again . . . my old man, who died, he was like you. A bum.'

'Now look –'

'Shut up, Fasher. My mum wanted to forget the name – so did I. Know what that name was, do you?'

Fasher wasn't looking quite so cocky now, Parsons thought, but he said, 'Tell me then I'll know.'

Parsons said, 'Never mind for now. Able Seaman, one good conduct badge that got lost when I went inside and had to be earned all over again. The charge was theft.'

Something had happened to Fasher's face now, but he didn't comment. Parsons' mind went back over the years, seeing again, vividly, the events of the past. Remembering how Holloway, too, had been intended to suffer aboard the *Sprinter* as a result of Fasher's nasty disposition. False evidence, like in his own years-old case – Fasher had specialized in that, and an AB's word didn't stand much chance against that of a PO. Especially a keen, zealous type like the erstwhile Petty Officer Fasher. Able Seaman Parsons had caught Petty Officer Fasher one fine day, or rather night, with his hand in the till of the barracks canteen: returning from liberty one summer evening he'd seen the act through a window and had seen also that Fasher had looked up at that moment and spotted him. Fasher had asked what he was gawping at, and Parsons had answered that he fancied he was watching theft. Fasher's face had tightened up and he'd said he was checking the cash, which was a stupid thing to say, since the cash was the concern of the canteen manager primarily and the Paymaster Commander of the barracks ultimately, and no one else. Fasher had ordered him to come inside and had then offered to split fifty-fifty if Parsons, Siddall as he then was, would keep his trap shut. When the refusal had come, Fasher had gone into action, shouted for the guard, and had Siddall arrested on a charge of rifling the canteen till. Siddall had been brought before the Officer of the Watch and been forwarded on as per routine to the

150

Commander and then the Commodore. He'd got detention and all that followed from that and he had known he would never ever make leading seaman. Theft was theft and spelled disgrace. It was only much later that he'd learned that the canteen manager, a NAAFI employee, had been checking some stocks and had witnessed the whole affair from start to finish and had heard all that Fasher had said. The manager had approached Fasher and told him this, foolishly; and Fasher had threatened to break him if he uttered thereafter. The canteen manager's name was unlikely to have been forgotten by Fasher, and now Parsons used it. The effect was electric. Fasher appeared to choke and his face went a deep red. Parsons said calmly, 'That NAAFI manager, he went ashore before the war started. He was a sick man – conscience, p'raps, I don't know. He's running a grocer's business now. I happened to meet him, not so long ago – on leave, I was. He's well outside your range now, Fasher, and he wants to make amends. Just in case he wasn't available if ever I needed him, he gave me a letter. That letter's with my mum. Sealed. If I kick the bucket at any time, she'll open it up and find instructions what to do.' He paused. 'I don't need to kick any buckets, not necessarily, to get it opened up and a copy forwarded to the Admiralty.'

Fasher's voice was scarcely audible. He said, 'You wouldn't bloody dare!'

'Wouldn't I? Just you try me and see, Fasher. I've been waiting . . . I always thought a day would come. I nearly bust a gut when I saw you come aboard to join. Now I reckon the time's come. The moment that letter goes in, you lose your bloody warrant, Fasher. You'll be out of the Andrew so fast your feet won't touch the ground, and then they'll call you up for the Army. A brown job. Private sodding Fasher, and bad bloody luck to you. That's if you come out of this. If you don't, you'll not go to an *oflag*. You'll live in pig shit in a *stalag* till the war's over and you come out to sod all.'

Fasher was trembling and now his face was white, as white as the snow that was still falling, spattering the train's windows. In a whisper, all fight gone from him, he asked,

151

'What is it you want, you bastard?'

Parsons grinned. 'Calling me names won't help, will it, Fasher? I want you to think about truth for the first time in your rotten life. This is for Holloway as well, see? Your draft to the *Sprinter* was the worst thing that ever happened to you, but I'm giving you the chance to make something decent out of it. I'm giving you the chance to show some guts. I reckon you know what I mean. The rest's up to you, Fasher.'

Parsons sat back, staring coolly at the Nazis. He could say no more now. As he'd said, it was up to Fasher. Fasher, no fool, would see it plain. He had to go right in and bugger up the Nazis' plans at Belomorsk, alert the Russians, and risk a bullet up the arse. He would know that Parsons and the rest would do what they could to back him inside the coach. He could get away with it; and if he did he would be a hero. If he died, it would be a hero's death. But if he didn't go along with Parsons, he would know the result of that as well. If the Nazis won out and he lived to become a POW for the duration, he would come out to disgrace and no pension. As Parsons had said: sod all.

Cameron felt more dead than alive by the time he reached the Russian official coach. He hadn't even the strength to turn the door handle; he simply held tight until he was seen through the glass. When that happened, the window alongside the door was lowered and helping hands grasped him and eased him through as the door was opened. For a while he sat slumped on a seat, and took some vodka from a flask, and gradually felt better. Then he told his story; two of the Russian officers spoke English reasonably well. There was a conference; some of the officers were for doing as Cameron had done – move along the step, and board the engine to have the train brought to a halt. The Nazis could then be taken before the train reached Belomorsk. But one of them knew the railway track better than the others.

'There are more tunnels between here and Belomorsk,' he said. 'The Englishman's plan is better. We shall leave the train immediately on arrival, and raise the alarm. I think

152

there will be little trouble, and a minimal loss of life. The Nazis cannot succeed now.'

Cameron believed that. But the Nazis were not going to give in easily and he feared very much more loss of life than the Russians seemed to imagine. And there was Yurigin: God alone could say what the Russian marshal would be facing after the Belomorsk arrival. Death, Siberia, disgrace; or perhaps he would surmount his difficulties and establish his loyalty. Cameron hoped he would; he had said nothing of the charges against Yurigin to the officers in the coach. He felt that was not his concern, and it was vital not to confuse the issue when the train pulled into the station.

Cameron looked from the windows, shivering at the memory of his nightmare progress along the step. The snowfall seemed to be heavier than ever and the train was slowing again from time to time. They were eventually going to get out into feet of the stuff, and movement along the platform would be slow: and the Russians were armed only with revolvers. Luck was still going to come into the picture. He looked at his watch: they still had some eight hours to go to Belomorsk.

The night passed with nerve-tearing slowness. It was still dark, still snowing but more lightly now, when the Russian who was familiar with the track said there was not much farther to go.

'About ten miles,' he said, looking intently from the window. They all sat in silence after that, their revolvers in their hands, all ready to move fast the moment the train slowed into the station. Soon they came to scattered buildings, the outskirts of Belomorsk. Cameron and the Russian officers got to their feet and stood by the coach doors; the women, the wives of the officers, had been told to remain in safety and to take cover behind the backs of the seats. They were not to emerge into the open until one of their menfolk came back and told them it was all clear.

In the forward coach where the Nazis were still in control, Able Seaman Parsons watched Fasher's face. It was working with fear and it was as yet uncertain which of his two fears

153

would come out on top. Parsons felt a looseness in his guts as the train began to slow for the run-in to the station. Within the next two or three minutes a lot of people's fates were going to be decided. The Nazi gunmen were moving for the doors now, ready to make their OGPU uniforms obvious when the station was reached.

As the train moved through the town's outskirts one of the gunmen beckoned to Fasher.

'You. To the door now. This one. Be very careful. Do exactly as you have been told. Nothing more, nothing less – you understand?'

Fasher's tongue came out to lick his lips. 'I understand,' he said. He met Parsons' sardonic eye and looked away again. Parsons saw that he was shaking like a leaf, as indeed he had shaken all through the night after their conversation. He moved to the door and took up his position.

The station came up alongside; the train slowed right down. One of the Nazis looked from a window. He said, 'There is a strong guard.'

'Transport?'

'Yes. Military vehicles alongside the track.'

There was a nod. 'Good! We shall succeed, never fear.' The face was set into hard lines of determination. None of the Nazi faces, Parsons had noted, were especially Germanic, at least not his idea of Jerries, square-heads . . . for one thing there were no give-away duelling scars. The gunmen had been well chosen; but the Jerries were always thorough. Parsons' heart was sinking; Fasher looked as though the threat of imminent death was getting the better of him. The thing could be brought off by the Nazis. If Fasher's nerve failed him then the Jerries had a pretty good chance of bulling their way through. There was a saying in the Andrew: BBB – Bullshit Baffles Brains. It did, too. If you were full enough of bull, you could get away with murder. The British services ran on it and no doubt the Russians were the same, just as susceptible.

With a clank of buffers the train ground to a halt and one of the Nazis swung open a door for Fasher. 'Now,' he said.

Fasher got down, ashen-faced. The OGPU uniform filled the doorway behind him. Behind the gunman's bulk the other two sub-machine-guns swung to keep the Naval ratings covered. From a window, Parsons watched. Fasher moved through the snow towards the Russian party. Then, through the opened door, Parsons heard some sort of panic, a diversion – shouts, in Russian. He shoved his head against the glass of the window, trying to see along the platform. A moment later he saw men running through the snow, saw that Mr Cameron was with them – in the lead was Cameron, moving as fast as the snow would let him. Fasher had turned his head towards the running men but was still moving on towards the welcoming committee. Just for a while. Then he stopped. Parsons saw him turn and point towards the coach. He shouted out; Parsons didn't catch the words. But the man in the OGPU uniform at the door suddenly brought his sub-machine-gun into view and fired a burst and Fasher fell, staggering, crashed into the bloodied snow and jerked and twitched for a moment and then lay still.

After that there was a murderous exchange of fire from both sides.

The survivors were feted that day in Belomorsk before being put aboard a train back to Murmansk. The British Navy had redeemed itself in Russian eyes, making up for the sinkings, the tragic loss of war supplies. The Russian leadership had been unctuously magnanimous about those losses and Cameron had managed to keep anger out of his voice as he responded. He was relieved when it was all over and they were Murmansk-bound. They were a much depleted party. The Nazis had kept up a murderous fire; the Russians had been forced to colander the coach. The gunner's mate was dead, so were three more seamen. All the remainder had been wounded, though none so seriously that they couldn't travel back to Murmansk under the care of a Russian doctor and nurse. Able Seaman Parsons was swathed in head bandages and his face was like a piece of parchment but he was perky enough. Cameron mentioned Fasher.

He said, 'Mr Fasher really saved the day, I believe. He gave us time, and took up the Germans' attention. It was a pretty good show.'

Parsons said,. 'That's right, sir.' There was no point in saying anything further. Death ironed out a lot of wrongs and whatever it was Fasher had been shouting when the bullets tore him apart didn't alter the fact that he was dead. Dead and travelling in a coach behind them, with a Russian guard of honour mounted. He would have the full show at his funeral; or maybe Mr Hawkey would want to give him a sea burial – he'd keep, in the interminable Russian snows. Well, let him have his moment of undeserved glory! The train rattled along; Parsons drifted off into sleep.

Not so Cameron; his mind was too busy. He would be glad to be back aboard; and he hoped Hawkey would be fit again by now. When the repairs had been completed and the *Sprinter* refuelled, they would be taking a convoy home, empty ships that would be filled again for Russia once they reached UK – which was why the Nazis would still be doing their best to stop them reaching a UK port, of course. The same thing all over again but in reverse. So it would go on, and on, and on . . . Cameron thought about Yurigin. The marshal had been whipped away after the shooting had stopped and Cameron hadn't seen him again, nor Harcourt Prynn either. Prynn, he had been told, had been driven straight to a conference, but there had been shrugs and silences when he'd enquired about Yurigin. During the afternoon a volley of rifle-fire had crashed out from a barrack yard; but it didn't *have* to be a firing squad.